## "Just what is   of this?"

This time Jake's g        b    c,
but broke, wide and devilish, in a flash of
white teeth in the moonlight.

"Oh, Mercedes, haven't you worked it out
yet? I would have thought that it was
obvious."

"Not to me it isn't," Mercedes snapped, her
voice tart with tension. "You'll have to spell
it out."

So he did.

"What I want out of this, Mercedes, my
darling, is you. I want you in my bed, as
my mistress. Always have done from the
first moment I saw you—and nothing has
changed. I want you, and I intend to get
you, one way or another."

# *The* *Alcolar Family*

*Proud, modern-day Spanish aristocrats—*
*passion is their birthright!*

Harlequin Presents® is proud to present
international bestselling author Kate Walker's
ALCOLAR FAMILY miniseries.

**Meet the Alcolar Family:**

**Joaquin:** The firstborn and only legitimate Alcolar
son. Can he forget his no-commitment rule and
make his twelve-month mistress his wife?
*The Twelve-Month Mistress* (#2492)

**Ramón:** The beloved illegitimate son, he gets
more than he bargained for in his carefully
planned marriage of convenience!
*The Spaniard's Inconvenient Wife* (#2498)

**Mercedes:** Can the only Alcolar daughter
find the man who is her match?
*Bound by Blackmail* (#2504)

Kate Walker is the author of more than
forty romance novels for Harlequin Presents®.
To find out about Kate, and her forthcoming
books, visit her Web site at www.kate-walker.com.

# Kate Walker

## BOUND BY BLACKMAIL

### The Alcolar Family

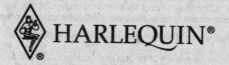

HARLEQUIN®

TORONTO • NEW YORK • LONDON
AMSTERDAM • PARIS • SYDNEY • HAMBURG
STOCKHOLM • ATHENS • TOKYO • MILAN • MADRID
PRAGUE • WARSAW • BUDAPEST • AUCKLAND

If you purchased this book without a cover you should be aware
that this book is stolen property. It was reported as "unsold and
destroyed" to the publisher, and neither the author nor the
publisher has received any payment for this "stripped book."

ISBN 0-373-12504-6

BOUND BY BLACKMAIL

First North American Publication 2005.

Copyright © 2005 by Kate Walker.

All rights reserved. Except for use in any review, the reproduction or
utilization of this work in whole or in part in any form by any electronic,
mechanical or other means, now known or hereafter invented, including
xerography, photocopying and recording, or in any information storage
or retrieval system, is forbidden without the written permission of the
publisher, Harlequin Enterprises Limited, 225 Duncan Mill Road,
Don Mills, Ontario, Canada M3B 3K9.

All characters in this book have no existence outside the imagination of
the author and have no relation whatsoever to anyone bearing the same
name or names. They are not even distantly inspired by any individual
known or unknown to the author, and all incidents are pure invention.

This edition published by arrangement with Harlequin Books S.A.

® and TM are trademarks of the publisher. Trademarks indicated with
® are registered in the United States Patent and Trademark Office, the
Canadian Trade Marks Office and in other countries.

www.eHarlequin.com

Printed in U.S.A.

# CHAPTER ONE

SO THAT was Mercedes Alcolar.

Jake lifted his glass to his lips and took a slow, thoughtful sip of the rich red wine it contained, swallowing it down without once taking his eyes off the woman who had just walked into the room.

Mercedes Honoria Alcolar.

The daughter of the great Catalan family at whose head was the world-renowned Juan Alcolar, owner and managing director of the Alcolar Corporation. This Mercedes was his youngest child, the only girl.

She was a looker all right. But then he'd expected that. How could she be anything else when her father was so much the traditional 'tall, dark and handsome' that he stole women's hearts if he so much as walked into a room? Her brothers did too, if the rumour mill was to be believed. Certainly, Ramón, his cousin and the one Alcolar he knew, was the sort of man who turned women's heads and always had been.

But Ramón was only this woman's half-brother. They shared the same father, but Ramón's mother had been Jake's aunt, and it was that thought that brought a dark scowl to his face as he watched the Alcolar girl progress across the room.

His mother couldn't speak the name Juan Alcolar without spitting venom. A venom she reserved for all the other members of the Alcolar clan—except, of course, Ramón. Because for years they hadn't known that Ramón was in fact an Alcolar. It was only ten years ago that they had discovered that he was the son, not of Reuben Dario, his aunt's husband, but of her lover, the man who had got her pregnant and then abandoned her—for the second time.

And that man had been Juan Alcolar.

'That man's daughter is coming to London,' Elizabeth Taverner had announced furiously the previous weekend when Jake had called to visit her for the evening.

'So I hear.'

He hadn't needed any further explanation as to who 'that man' was. There was no one else that Elizabeth referred to in that way and with just that bitter emphasis.

'I understand that Antonia Sanders has said she'll show her round—take her to a couple of parties.'

His mother's blonde head turned sharply in Jake's direction, eyes as blue as her son's flashing sharply.

'Parties you'll be going to?'

'Parties I'll be going to,' Jake confirmed a trifle wearily. 'But I doubt if I'll meet the girl, and even if I do… Mother, it's *years* since all that happened—a lifetime.'

'A lifetime my sister never had,' Elizabeth reminded him bitterly, her long, manicured fingers tapping restlessly on the gold brocade arm of the settee on which she sat. 'Marguerite *died* because of that man!'

'We don't know that for sure…'

'The doctors said—'

'The doctors said that Aunt Marguerite had a weak heart; one that was made worse by the strain of pregnancy and childbirth—'

'They can call it a weak heart, but to my mind she died because her heart was *broken*—and broken twice by the same man!'

Jake privately doubted that anyone could die of a broken heart, but he bit his tongue and held back the comment now. It would only aggravate his mother's mood, set her off on a tirade of anger and loathing that he had heard so many times before that he was frankly tired of it.

'Well, I doubt very much that I'll meet the woman, even if we do go to the same parties. And besides, I've kept away from her and her family for years now—I'm not likely to go rushing in to say hello just because we've discovered we're not-quite-related by marriage.'

'I should hope not. Certainly not after the way that her papa handled that takeover bid.'

Another black mark against Juan Alcolar, Jake reflected now, still watching Mercedes Alcolar, in spite of himself.

She was intensely watchable, that was the problem. Average height, but slim as a willow—apart from the rich, soft curves of her breasts under the clinging red and black dress. Her slightly olive skin looked soft and velvety, her oval face was enhanced by deep brown, almond-shaped eyes fringed by luxuriant black lashes above incredible slanting cheekbones and a lush, full mouth that barely needed the slick of lipstick to colour it more richly. Silken black hair was twisted into a neat knot at the base of her skull, leaving the whole of her long, elegant neck exposed, her only jewellery the cascade of silver that hung from the delicate lobe of each finely shaped ear.

But it was the way she moved that caught his eye—and held it. She was sleek and sophisticated, walking with the elegance of a female cat, the sway of her hips, the slide of the long, slim legs a sensual temptation that kicked low and hard in his gut.

Of course, she wasn't to blame for the way her father had behaved, either in the past or more recently when a hostile takeover bid that Juan Alcolar had launched for a firm that Jake had had his eye on had caused a couple of very rocky years for Taverner Telecommunications. The company had been in danger of losing a lot of money and as a result, reluctantly, he had had to lay off staff.

And Juan Alcolar hadn't given a damn.

'No...' Jake muttered to himself, draining the last of his

wine and replacing his glass on the nearest table. 'I'm not interested.'

Mercedes Alcolar might be the most beautiful woman he had seen in years—in his life—but if she was anything like her father then she spelled trouble.

She spelled trouble anyway, whatever she was like. His mother would hit the roof if she thought that he had even spoken to the girl, let alone found her attractive. And no doubt her father would feel the same. Everything he had ever heard about the man spoke of an unbending arrogance, a pride in his Catalan heritage, his position in society, that kept him distant from the common herd of humanity.

It was as he was turning away, planning on heading for the door, that something caught his eye, made him glance back, his searching gaze meeting the wide, dark chocolate eyes of Mercedes Alcolar head on.

Just for a moment their eyes locked; held. He couldn't look away and neither—it seemed—could she. She looked like a startled fawn frozen into stillness by some sudden disturbing sound, staring, unblinking, straight at him.

But then she blinked and suddenly her whole face changed. The stunned look vanished, evaporating like a mist before the sun, and a totally different expression took its place.

If he hadn't known that she was still standing there, and that he had been watching her all the time, Jake might almost have believed that someone else had come into the room and taken her place. Her beautiful, expressive features simply froze, a cold masklike look settling over them as if they had suddenly become formed in ice. Her sensual lips stiffened, tightened into a thin, hard line, and her neat chin came up so that she was suddenly looking at him down the slope of her aristocratic, straight little nose.

Even the glorious shining brown eyes seemed to glaze over and turn icy, cold and distant as the rocks at the bottom of the sea on a bitter winter's day.

And, seeing it, Jake felt as if something of the cold, or a splinter of ice, had slid into his heart right then and there. Mercedes Alcolar might be the most beautiful woman he had ever seen but, right now, she also looked like the coldest, the haughtiest, the most arrogant female he had ever had the misfortune to encounter.

And who the hell are *you*? that look seemed to say. Who are you and how dare you even look in my direction?

Her father had looked that way on the one occasion that Jake had actually come close enough to see him. They had both attended some media function in a huge Madrid hotel and something had displeased Juan Alcolar. Some question that an enquiring reporter had asked had annoyed him and he had turned just that sort of a 'Who the hell are you?' look on the unfortunate man before turning and walking out without another word.

And who the hell are you, to look at me like that, Señorita Alcolar? He addressed the Spanish woman in the privacy of his thoughts. Don't you know that we dropped the feudal system here centuries ago? You may be aristocracy in Spain—but here you're just ordinary.

Oh, you liar! his senses reproached him, something twisting sharply inside him. You total, abject liar! Never in a million years could this woman be described as *ordinary*, not even as the worst possible term of disparagement. She was *gorgeous*—but the trouble was that she knew it.

And he was determined that he wouldn't let her see how she affected him. That down-the-nose look, the icy stare, told him that she was only too well aware of the effect she had on men, and only condescended to acknowledge it when it suited her. And this time it obviously didn't suit.

Quite deliberately he let his eyes flick over her once, up and down, then away again, as if totally uninterested. Not even sparing her another glance, he turned on his heel and walked swiftly away. The brief, twenty-stride journey to the

door seemed to last for ever, but he refused to let himself
even hesitate, fighting a nasty little battle with the almost
overwhelming urge to look back, just once, to see how she
had taken his dismissal of her.

If that was Mercedes Alcolar, then he wanted nothing to
do with her.

'Oh, damn!' Mercedes muttered under her breath, furious
with herself and the stupid way she had reacted. 'Damn,
damn, damn!'

She'd done it again. Gone and behaved in that ridiculous,
stupid way that always seemed to take over her at the worst
possible moment. Always, when she was at her most unsure
and uncomfortable, when she felt ill at ease and like a fish
out of water, then her wretched, stupid face had to go and
freeze up like that the minute anyone looked at her.

She knew what she looked like. She had caught sight of
herself just once, in a huge, ornate mirror overhanging the
large fireplace in her father's dining room, and she had been
horrified—appalled. Had that cold-faced, cold-eyed creature
really been her? It had to have been—the woman she'd been
able to see had been wearing the same dress as she had, had
had her hair in the same style. And yet the woman in the
reflection had looked icily haughty, arrogant as hell, and she
had most definitely looked as if she'd been determined to
freeze out anyone who'd approached her.

The reality couldn't have been more different.

The truth was that deep inside she had been scared stiff.
She had never been at her best at social gatherings, and the
bigger they were, the more she quailed inside.

And this event was *big*.

'Everybody who is anybody will be there!' Antonia had
announced as they had dressed and primped beforehand,
struggling for space in the tiny bathroom of her friend's one
bedroomed flat. 'Marlon and Heidi throw such wicked par-

ties! You'll really see some of the big names in the media world.'

Which was guaranteed to set Mercedes' nerves fluttering even before they left the house.

'You will stick with me, won't you, Tonia?' she asked just as the taxi drew up outside the huge, imposing entrance and the car door was opened by a uniformed servant. 'You won't leave me alone?'

'Of course not!' Her friend laughed. 'But don't worry— this is going to be *fun*!'

Fun for Antonia, perhaps, Mercedes thought to herself, struggling to stick close to her friend as the other girl made her way through a series of enormous rooms, each of them more crowded than the next. Occasionally Antonia stopped to introduce her to someone, but the buzz of conversation was so loud, the crush of people constantly shifting and moving around her, that Mercedes barely even registered whom she was speaking to, let alone their names, before they moved on again.

To make matters worse, she knew she was not really understanding half of what was said. Good as her English was, it wasn't really up to coping with the shouted questions, the laughing comments, all pitched against the beat of the music and the clatter of glasses.

And it was just when she was feeling her worst that she looked up and saw the man leaning against the far wall.

Alex.

Her first thought was that he looked like her brother Alex. But then realisation dawned and she knew that Alex could never be here—and, besides, this man wasn't really that much like him.

He was tall and rangy with dark brown hair and his eyes, what she could see of them because they were narrowed in sharp assessment, seemed blue, or something light that was not what she expected. But still, it was just some momentary trick of the light, or his height, or his colouring that had made her think of Alex. Because everything about this man told her that he was not *like* anyone. That he was totally, uniquely himself.

And what he was was stunning. Dark and devastating and wholly male in a way that made him stand out from the crowds of beautiful people all around her.

'Tonia?'

She reached for her friend's arm, wanting to draw her attention.

'Who...?'

But then the words shrivelled on her lips as she saw that he was staring straight at her.

It wasn't just that he was looking in her direction, but something about the *way* that he was doing so—some coldness in his demeanour, a frown between the narrowed eyes—that made her freeze. Her skin prickled with awareness, the tiny hairs on the back of her neck seeming to lift in wary response to that assessing frown.

Immediately her defence mechanisms came into play.

She didn't know who the man was—or why he was staring at her like that. She only knew that she wasn't going to let him outface her—that she was determined not to show, for a single second, the way that he affected her.

The way that he *disturbed* her.

She could feel her face tightening as if the skin had dried and were stretching taut over bone. Instinctively, she firmed her jaw, the movement clamping her mouth a little too much. Her head came up, chin lifting, in defiance.

And it had totally the wrong effect.

To her horror she saw the way his own expression hardened suddenly; the scathing contempt in the look that seared over her from head to toe and back up again.

She felt judged by that look. Judged and found wanting,

and totally, absolutely dismissed as being not worth any interest at all.

And even as she recognised that fact, he turned and stalked away, leaving her shaking as if that burning look had had an actual physical effect on her, draining the strength from her legs, stripping away a protective layer of skin. She felt raw and vulnerable, and badly upset—and the worst part was that she had no idea why.

'Mercedes?'

It was Tonia's voice, breaking into her miserable and shaken mood.

'You okay?'

'Oh—yes—fine.'

She switched on a bright, vivid smile, one she hoped was convincing, pushing the memory of that cold, dismissive stare right to the back of her mind.

She would forget him, she told herself. Forget him completely and never let him trouble her again. She only had another week here in England, and she wasn't going to let some unknown man spoil her trip for her.

Because this might be her only brief knowledge of what real freedom meant. The freedom of being away from the rules and restrictions of Spanish society life.

While she was here, she knew that she was supposed to be thinking of her future—or, rather, the future that Miguel Hernandez and his family hoped she would consider.

She and Miguel had dated for a while and he at least had clearly hoped to take the relationship a lot further. Her father approved of him too, she knew. The Hernandez family was wealthy, established in business, eminently respectable. She could do much worse for herself—*Papá* hadn't actually spoken the words out loud, but she had seen them in his eyes when he had spoken of Miguel. But even more revealing had been the expression on the faces of both of Miguel's parents. For their son to marry the only daughter of Juan Alcolar would clearly be a dream come true to them. In their eyes she was the perfect potential daughter-in-law—a prize catch.

Which had been why she had escaped to England on the pretext of taking time to think things over. Feeling the need to escape from the pressure of being viewed like a prize mare in a breeding programme, and not at all sure that her own feelings for Miguel could ever be anything more than warm affection, she had been enjoying herself so much in London—up until now.

'Mercedes. Look.' Antonia tugged at her friend's arm, distracting her attention. 'Over there—that's…'

In the noisy hubbub of voices, Mercedes missed the name, but looking where directed she recognised the handsome, clean-cut features of the latest English film sensation who had just come into the room, a petite, glamorous blonde on his arm.

'Isn't he just *gorgeous*!' Antonia sighed, almost drooling into her champagne glass.

A noncommittal, 'Mmm,' was all that Mercedes could manage. Anything more, and she'd have to explain herself. And right now explaining was not something she wanted to do.

*The man*—because even in her thoughts the words seemed to appear in italics—was back. Unexpectedly he had come back into the room and was leaning against the wall some distance away. And he was watching her again. She could feel the burn of his gaze on her skin even though she didn't dare to look in his direction.

'Not my type,' she added reluctantly when her friend clearly expected her to say something.

'You're joking—then who is? Oh, 'Cedes, not him!'

It escaped on a sound of shock and disbelief as Mercedes made the tiniest nodding gesture towards the tall, dark man in the elegantly tailored steel-grey suit. His attention had now been distracted by some glamorous redhead, Mercedes was

relieved to note. So for the moment at least she could look
without risk.

'Why not?' she asked sharply. 'Is he married?'

'No way!'

Antonia's expression said it all.

'That's Jake Taverner. Jake "Taverner Telecommunications"
Taverner,' she elaborated when Mercedes looked genuinely
blank, the name meaning nothing to her. 'Also known as Jake
"Marriage is not for me" Taverner.'

'My brother said that once.'

Mercedes smiled, her thoughts going to Joaquin's recent
wedding—the announcement that he and his wife Cassie
were expecting their first child.

'He changed his mind.'

'Well, I don't see Jake T changing his. For one thing, no
one seems to stay around long enough to have any chance
of influencing him. I heard he ditched...'

The words trailed off, Antonia's expression changing
abruptly. And the way she stared briefly, then hurriedly
looked away again, sent shivers of nervous apprehension running down Mercedes' spine.

''Cedes,' she whispered out of the corner of her mouth,
'don't look now—but he's coming over—he's heading
straight for us!'

# CHAPTER TWO

JAKE had told himself that he was going to stay away. Right away.

Mercedes Alcolar was trouble with a capital T.

If he hadn't known that from the simple fact of who she was and her connection to the family that his mother detested; to the man who she claimed had ruined her sister's life—and so her own—then that 'who the hell are you?' look would have made things plain to him without any words being spoken.

She was trouble, and he had no intention of stirring up the hornets' nest that any further acquaintance with her might involve.

But somehow he couldn't keep to that resolve.

Just one glimpse of her and she had got under his skin. Her image was there in his mind, and he couldn't get free of it. Couldn't erase her from his thoughts, or distract himself with anything else.

And he tried.

He tried drink, but the vintage champagne might have been ordinary tap water for all the effect it had on him.

He tried flirting. There was plenty of opportunity to talk with some of the most beautiful women in the world, and most of them seemed only too happy to have his attention for as long as they could.

But their attractions palled surprisingly quickly. And he found that when he talked to them, it wasn't their face he saw but the delicate, fine-boned features and big dark eyes of Mercedes Alcolar.

But he wasn't going to do anything about it, he told him-

self. He most definitely was not going back into the main
ballroom where she still lingered with her friend. He wasn't
that stupid.

He thought he'd managed to convince himself. He stayed
that way right up until the moment that he found himself
back in the middle of a crowded room, scanning the guests
for one particular face.

And when he spotted it he felt as if he had come home.

'So you've seen our exotic little Spanish visitor.' The man
he had been talking to—a man whose name he couldn't even
remember—made the remark as his eyes drifted over the
slender but shapely body, the gleaming hair...

Only the most beautiful woman with the most perfect features could take the severe way that she wore her hair,
scraped back from her face and pinned up. On Mercedes
Alcolar it looked stunning, but still the sudden urgent need
to unpin it, to let it fall down around her shoulders, feel it
brush his face, was a painful twist in his gut.

'Gorgeous, isn't she?'

He supposed he said yes—or maybe just made an inartic-
ulate sound that the other man could take as agreement if he
wanted. But he didn't really know and he didn't care.
Because without being rationally aware of having made a
decision, suddenly he was moving, making his way across
the room, weaving between groups by instinct because he
wasn't looking anywhere but at that face.

She saw him coming.

She looked up and those big dark eyes fixed on his face
as she watched him walk towards her. And his throat tightened as he waited to see that change come over her expression once again. Waited to see her features freeze, her chin
come up...

It didn't happen. Her face didn't change at all.

Instead she just watched—a little warily, her eyes slightly

hooded. But she didn't freeze him out, and he didn't know whether to feel relief or regret at that.

Relief at the thought that she wasn't going to cut him dead, refuse to speak to him, spurn him without a second's consideration. Regret at the realisation that now nothing could stop this. He was set on a course of action that had to be followed through, no matter what. He didn't care if his mother—and the rest of her family—went crazy over this. He didn't give a damn as to what the Alcolars might think either.

He had to meet this woman, or go quietly mad somewhere.

'Tonia…'

Someone spoke and he realised that it was her. Mercedes Alcolar had let the single word slip from her lips, even though she hadn't taken her eyes off his face as she reached out to touch her friend's arm, in a strangely almost defensive gesture.

'Toneeya…' she had said and the soft, faintly husky voice, the slightly alien pronunciation, had turned the familiar name into a very different sound.

Her voice was as beautiful as everything else about her.

'You're Mercedes Alcolar.'

It came out baldly, bluntly, but that was what had been uppermost in his mind. She was Mercedes Alcolar and he wanted above all else to get to know her.

'Sì.'

Mercedes winced inside as she heard the shivering, fragile thread that her voice had become. She sounded weak and defenceless, a maidservant responding to her master, and she had no idea why.

When she had seen him coming towards her, she had been determined to get a grip on herself. This time, she vowed, she wouldn't make the same mistake. This time she wouldn't freeze him out—give him another excuse to turn his back on her and walk away, dismissing her from his thoughts.

She had made herself face him. Had even tried for a smile

though that had been too much. So she had just watched him come. The look in his light eyes, the determined set of the strong jaw, had dried her mouth, making her heart race, setting up a disturbed and uneven pulse in her throat so that when she had tried to whisper to Tonia it had come out much louder than she'd expected.

But now her voice seemed to have died.

Something had happened to her in the moment that he had spoken to her.

'You're Mercedes Alcolar,' he had said.

The deep, rich voice couldn't have come from anyone else, Mercedes told herself, fighting hard against revealing the way that shivers of awareness were running down the exposed line of her spine. She had never been particularly attracted to the English accent before, finding it too clipped and hard to be truly appealing. But this man's voice made her think of dark, warm honey, and she knew a sudden, ridiculous feeling that she had been waiting all her life to hear him speak her name and know how it would sound on his tongue.

She felt her toes curl inside her shoes at the sound.

He didn't, as most English speakers she had met, put a hard 'ee' sound into it, but used the Spanish pronunciation perfectly, the word whispering across her skin like a caress. Involuntarily she smiled in quick response and saw the answering light in his eyes.

'That's right. My name is Mercedes Alcolar.'

She saw his head tilt slightly in acknowledgement of the name, and those silvery blue eyes lingered on her face, darkening in appreciation.

'And I am Jake Taverner,' he said. 'You are related to Juan Alcolar—of the Alcolar Corporation.'

It took a second or two for Mercedes to realise that he had framed the words as a statement, not as a question, but by that time she had already responded with an affirmative nod.

'He's my father.'

Jake's dark head went back slightly and the smile that flashed on and off had an element in it that worried her faintly just for a second. In fact, there was something about this man that made her senses flash in red alarm, but for no good reason that she could see.

She got an impression of strength held back, of feelings ruthlessly reined in, and the rigid control under the natural, and dangerously appealing, charm unnerved her.

'Would you like a drink, Mercedes Alcolar? Or perhaps to dance?'

'I don't think you mean that.'

The words slipped out before she could catch them back, betraying her inner apprehension and making him frown intimidatingly.

'Don't mean what?'

'The—invitation to dance,' Mercedes managed, painfully aware of the way that Antonia was staring at her, goggle-eyed, unable to believe the way she was behaving.

'And why would I not mean that?'

'I got the impression…'

Oh, how did she explain this?

*I have a strange feeling…*

Or.

*I sense there's something you're not saying…*

Or just plain downright simply:

*There's something about you that scares me.*

He was waiting for an answer. Waiting quietly and apparently patiently, with just the faintest, indecipherable smile on his face, and that simple fact made a nonsense of all her fears. And yet she couldn't quite shake them off.

'I thought that—earlier…' She hesitated, and saw his expression change yet again, a new light coming into those blue eyes as, like her, he recalled the way he had reacted when she had first seen him.

'Earlier I was a fool,' he said. 'A bad mood—nothing more.'

'And now you're no longer in a bad mood?'

That was better. She sounded a little more human; a little more like herself.

And Jake Taverner obviously thought so too as a wide, stunning grin suddenly flashed across his face. It made her blink in shock, take a half-step backwards, adjusting awkwardly as she tried to regain her balance.

Immediately his hand shot out, caught her by the elbow, held her steady. And the feeling was like nothing she had ever known. The touch of his hand on her bare arm, hard, hot palm against soft, sensitive skin, sent a feeling like a flash of lightning rushing through every nerve, making them come alive and sizzle with sensation.

'I only have one hour of being a fool in a year. Unfortunately, you happened to hit on it. It won't happen again.'

'Not for another year?'

'No— So now you have three hundred and sixty four days when I'm going to be totally sensible. So will you dance with me?'

Behind his back, Mercedes could see out the corner of her eye that Antonia was gesticulating wildly, nodding a frantic encouragement to say yes. But her friend's face, the rest of the room, and all the people in it had blurred and all she could see was a lean, stunningly masculine face and a pair of burning blue eyes that held her own brown gaze with mesmeric power.

'All right,' she said slowly, a new strength and conviction coming back into her voice. 'Yes, I'll dance with you.'

From then on the night took on the feeling of a dream. A dream in which the most devastating man in the room concentrated all his attention on her, leaving no one in any doubt that she had caught his interest, held it—and he was not about to let anyone else muscle in on his territory.

The dance was part of the dream—that first dance, and then all of the rest, so many that she lost count in the end.

She only knew that in his arms she felt like someone else. She felt new and reborn—and yet totally herself. Her skin sang at his touch on the bare flesh of her arms, her hands, the line of her back exposed by the dip of the dress. Her blood heated in her veins and her heart danced along with the faster rhythms of the music. And at the end of the evening, when the tempo slowed and he gathered her close, she rested her cheek against his shoulder, breathing in the warm scent of his skin, the faint tang of some subtle, citrusy aftershave, and felt as though she were dancing on air, her feet not even touching the ground.

If he would just kiss her—even only once—then the evening would be perfect, she told herself. She wouldn't ask for anything more. Wouldn't even hope for another night such as this. Just one kiss, and she could be happy with that.

When the end of the evening came Jake walked with her and Antonia to the taxi that her friend had ordered to collect them, and offered only a cool, perfectly decorous goodnight, helping her into her seat with courtesy but no apparent regret. But before he shut the door, he lifted a hand and touched a gentle fingertip to Mercedes' cheek. Just a single, soft caress, and then it was gone, leaving the skin feeling suddenly cold and strangely empty where his finger had once been.

'I'll see you again,' he said.

Not, 'Can I see you again?' or, 'When can I see you again?' but 'I'll see you.' And then he turned and walked away, disappearing into the crowd, while Mercedes was still gaping, trying to get her breath, wanting to say, 'But you haven't got my number.'

By the time the words would form, the taxi was already pulling away and Mercedes could only twist in her seat and look back, staring at the space where he had been, struggling vainly for one last sight of him.

He had to put a hold on this somehow, Jake told himself as he forced his feet to walk away, forced his head not to turn, forced his eyes to stare straight ahead, and not even look back, not once. Because if he looked back then he was lost. He had to pull on the brakes—or at least slow down the feeling that he was in a runaway train that was careering down the steepest hill around.

He had known that he was in trouble from the moment that he had found that he was walking towards her when every instinct had warned that he should be moving in the opposite direction. The Alcolar family and his should stay at the distance they had always maintained until now. But, for Jake, the problem had become much more personal.

He should never have touched her.

It wasn't enough. The feel of the satin warmth of the soft skin of her arm under his hand was a tormenting temptation, never, ever enough. And to hold her in his arms as they had danced, to feel the curves of her body pressed up against his, had aroused him so fiercely, making him rock-hard in the space of a heartbeat.

By the time the dance had ended, he had been literally shaking with need, as stunned and horny as an adolescent at his first experience of the delights of the female body. So much so that he had been thankful when the music had ended and they could move apart.

But as soon as they were apart he had known that this feeling was worse. He had had to have Mercedes in his arms, had wanted to hold her, had needed to hold her. And so when the music had started up again he had reached for her, held her, danced with her, putting himself through the same torture all over again—because being without it had been worse.

That was why he hadn't been able to stay around and watch her be driven away. He hadn't even been able to kiss her goodnight because if he had done then he would never have stopped at one kiss. His still-aching body would have demanded more—so much more—right here, right now.

'Hellfire and damnation!'

Jake reached into his jacket pocket, pulled out his cell phone and flicked it open, pressing a speed-dial number with his thumb.

'Jessie? Sorry to trouble you at this time but I have something I need you to do for me. Antonia Sanders—the girl who works for Anchor Radio—do you have her details? I need her address...'

# CHAPTER THREE

'YOU have precisely fifteen minutes in which to change if you want to.'

Not having her phone number had proved to be no problem to Jake Taverner, Mercedes found. He hadn't troubled with ringing her or asking her out again. Instead he had simply turned up on her doorstep the next night, with an invitation to dinner.

No, invitation wasn't the right word. He had delivered what was more of an ultimatum. Dinner with him—or nothing.

And having spent the whole night dreaming about him, the day struggling to get her thoughts onto anything else but Jake Taverner, *nothing* was all she would be left with if she turned down his suggestion.

She'd made the fifteen minutes by the skin of her teeth, throwing off her jeans and tee shirt and pulling on a pale pink and white spotted sundress in their place. A smudge of eyeshadow, a single coat of mascara, and a slick of lip gloss and she was ready. Though she might as well have not bothered for all the comment Jake made when she reappeared. He seemed more interested in getting her out of the house, and away from Antonia's obvious excited interest.

'Where are we going?' she asked a trifle breathlessly when she was in the car and they were pulling away from the house in which Antonia had her flat. 'What restaurant?'

'No restaurant. I had caterers prepare a meal at my place.'

Her silence clearly said things he didn't want to hear because he turned sharply, frowning faintly.

'Is that a problem?'

'N—no.'

Mercedes struggled to sound convincing. She was in England now, not Spain, she told herself. Antonia had already made it plain that she thought the carefully controlled existence Mercedes accepted as normal was positively archaic in her mind.

'You've never even slept with a man!' she had exclaimed when, over a late-night glass of wine, Mercedes had admitted her lack of experience in such things. 'But I thought you were practically engaged!'

'Miguel's family and mine have—an understanding,' Mercedes explained. 'They would like to see us married—but Miguel has not proposed yet, and I haven't given him any promises.'

'And you haven't…'

Antonia's expressively raised eyebrows left no words needing to be said.

'No, we haven't! It's not the same in my country as it is here. We've kissed, of course…and cuddled…'

'Well,' her friend returned archly, 'then you'd better stop dreaming about Jake Taverner, sweetie. Believe me, he's not the sort of guy to be satisfied with a kiss and a cuddle.'

But what Antonia didn't know, Mercedes thought to herself with a small secret smile, was that with Jake Taverner she too didn't think she could be satisfied with a kiss and a cuddle.

In his arms on the dance floor, she had felt the flowering of a whole new set of sensations deep within her body. For the first time in her life she had known something of what it really meant to be a woman; something that none of Miguel's awkward kissing and clumsy fumblings had ever aroused. She had sensed the uncoiling of some raw, primitive need low down in her pelvis, the sudden heat between her legs. At once she had known what people meant when they talked about hot desire or hunger or simply need. She had felt those things in Jake's arms and he had been the first man to awaken those sorts of feelings in her.

'What's that smile for?' Jake startled her by asking. She had been convinced that his full attention was on driving through the crowded London streets, but clearly he had caught the brief expression as it had crossed her face.

'Wouldn't you like to know?'

'I intend to find out.'

'You can try!'

Mercedes amazed herself with her sudden newfound ability to flirt, casting a wicked sidelong glance at his face, secretly admiring the hard, carved lines of his profile etched against the car window. There was a sensation like fizzing champagne inside her stomach, intoxicating her, exhilarating.

And she knew what it was. It was freedom.

It was the fact that she was here, in London, on her own, liberated, independent, as Antonia was. She was no longer in Spain, living life the way her father wanted her to, following his rules, living according to his standards.

She had never realised before just how heavy and ponderous those rules were. Never seen how restricted and confined her life had been.

In Spain she would never have been to a party like the ones Antonia had taken her to. She would never, ever, have met anyone like Jake Taverner. The idea made her giddy with excitement and anticipation.

'But you might have to force it out of me.'

'Oh, I don't think I'll need to do that.'

Jake's laughter was low and sensual.

'I can think of other ways that I could use to persuade you.'

That laughter sent a thrill like an electric current running down her spine and tingling low in her body at just the thought of what he might mean.

'What sorts of ways?'

The car had pulled up at a red traffic light and Jake took the opportunity to slant a wicked, mocking glance in her direction.

'I'm sure I can find something...'

There was a promise and a threat in his tone, one that combined with the already volatile combination of emotions fizzing inside her to create a potentially explosive mixture, one in which she didn't know whether apprehension, excitement or sheer blind fear was uppermost.

'I'm sure you can.'

The lights changed as she spoke and Jake eased the car forward. The movement of his feet on the clutch and accelerator pedals made the long muscles in his powerful thighs clench and release in a way that made Mercedes' blood heat, her throat dry. The sense of liberation and exhilaration was enticing, intoxicating, and she couldn't resist it.

Reaching out, she touched a light hand to the denim-covered strength of his thigh, meaning only to press it lightly, then dodge away again. But the feeling of the rough material, the heat and tightness of the muscles underneath it, drove all sense and caution from her brain.

She let her fingers rest more firmly, lingering, smoothing the raised seam of his jeans with a slightly unsteady movement, and felt his leg jerk, heard the swiftly indrawn breath in response.

'Do you know what you're doing, little lady?'

'I can guess.'

She sounded much more provocative than she felt.

She didn't know—not really, not fully. But she suspected. And the realisation that she could have this sort of effect on this sort of a man—a man like Jake Taverner; a real man, beside whom poor Miguel would just look like a boy—went straight to her head like a rush of rich, potent wine.

'Don't you like it?'

His response was another of those low, deep chuckles, a sound that sent a thrill shivering through her.

'I like it. It's just I might like it too much for what I have in mind tonight.'

'And what is that?'

'And watteezdat?' Jake mimicked her accent and the pronunciation that a sudden jolting rush of nerves had made less accurate than she could normally manage. 'Why, dinner, of course—what else did you think?'

Was she really as innocent as she looked? he had to wonder, seeing the sudden rush of colour that flooded into her cheeks. Which one was the real Mercedes? The proud, haughty beauty who had turned such cold eyes on him in the first moment that she had seen him; the consummate flirt who had destroyed his composure in a second, with the lightest touch on his leg; or the apparently flustered young girl who had suddenly blushed at his teasing?

He was going to enjoy finding out. The only problem was going to be keeping his hands off her long enough to really get to know her.

That stroking caress along his thigh had had the effect of sending a lightning bolt through his body, making him so hot and hungry that he was not really safe to be in control of the car. All he could think of was the way that the flimsy pink dress had ridden up high on her legs as she sat in the car, revealing long, slender thighs covered in the finest silk.

Tights or stockings?

Stockings, he'd be willing to bet. Slithery, lace-topped stockings that...

Oh, hell, no! The hot surge of erotic pleasure at just the thought damaged his concentration, making his hands on the wheel slip just for a second.

He had to get a grip—both mentally and physically—or they would both end up in the gutter, rather than the deep, sensual bed where his sexual imaginings had taken them.

He was going to concentrate hard on other things. He had to, or the evening would be over before it began.

Much as he wanted to take this woman to bed, the fact that she was who she was brought complications that could make one night with her cost much more than he was ever prepared to pay. It was much better to play things safe—take them one step at a time—and make sure that he was not setting up potential problems for himself by making a move before he had checked out all the possible complications first.

It wasn't easy but he managed to keep his hands off her through most of the meal. But the problem was that Mercedes Alcolar was temptation personified. Her smile, her laugh, the sensual movements of her body, the waft of her perfume on the air, all whispered enticement to his hungry senses. The way she ate, her enjoyment of the food the caterers had provided, was pure seduction in itself. He had found himself leaning forward more and more, taking every opportunity to refill her glass, offer her a taste of something particularly good, once even wiping a speck of rich, creamy sauce from the spot where it lay along the soft, luscious curve of her lip.

And Mercedes moved closer and closer. Always on some pretext or other—so that he could reach her glass better—to move away from the spot where some water had spilled… But she had ended up sitting *next* to him, just at the corner of the table—very, very close instead of opposite him.

And then he was unable to hold back any longer. Giving in to the primitive urgings that had been pulsing in his blood ever since she had opened the door to him, he leaned forward and pressed a long, lingering kiss on the tempting red mouth that still glistened with the shine left by the coating of sauce.

She blinked, just once, closing her chocolate-coloured eyes for a moment before opening them again and looking straight into his.

'What was that for?' she asked, her low, musical voice suddenly unexpectedly husky and uneven.

\*    \*    \*

If the truth was told, Mercedes admitted to herself, she had just decided that she'd got this all wrong. She'd been reading the signs badly, misinterpreting his words, his actions.

She had stupidly, idiotically convinced herself that Jake Taverner was really, truly interested in her as a woman, when it seemed that he was anything but.

She'd done everything she could to encourage him. She'd smiled, flirted, teased. She'd laughed at all his jokes, listened attentively to all his stories, gazed into his eyes across the candle-lit table. She had even deliberately moved closer on the slightest pretext, actually knocking her water glass so that it had spilled and soaked into the cloth where she sat, so that she'd had to take her chair several stages round the table— in Jake's direction.

And it had got her precisely nowhere.

He had been polite, amusing, considerate—but nothing more than that. He had made sure that she'd had everything she wanted to eat, poured her wine with a generous hand, concentrated flatteringly on everything she had said—but she was sure that he would do that for anyone.

He seemed to have pulled back from her, to have withdrawn into himself, and that was not what she wanted. The special looks he had given her on the night they had met, the way that those blue, blue eyes had lingered on her face, or had watched her when she'd moved, had been switched off. He didn't touch her, let alone hold her in the way that he had done when they'd been dancing, and that deep, rich voice, with its intriguing accent, didn't sound like a physical caress any more. Instead, it was cool, calm, controlled.

And she didn't want calm, cool and controlled. She wanted freedom and excitement and wildness. She wanted to get back the feeling she had felt in those moments in his arms on the dance floor. She wanted to experience them all over again—but this time in the privacy of Jake's home so that

she could see how far they could take them; learn just where
those incredible sensations could lead.

'Did it have to be *for* anything?' Jake answered her. 'I
wanted to do it. Why? Didn't you like it?'

She actually pretended to consider for a moment, still holding his gaze locked with hers, and she knew that he saw the
light that gleamed in the darkness of her eyes—a gleam that
spoke of sexual provocation, of deliberate teasing.

Slowly, sensuously, she slid out the pink tip of her tongue
and slicked it over her moist lips, absorbing the taste of his
kiss, and enjoying it all over again.

'Oh, yes, I liked it,' she murmured. 'It was—nice. But
somehow I was hoping for something rather more than *nice*.'

'Oh, were you? And what, exactly, were you hoping for?
Something like this?'

Leaning across the corner of the table, he crushed his
mouth to hers again, more firmly this time, taking her lips
with a pressure that had them parting under his so that he
could run the tip of his tongue along her mouth, caressing
and tantalising the moist inner cleft.

'O-h-h...' Mercedes responded as he slowly moved back,
away from her, and she pressed her fingers to her mouth as
if to hold the lingering memory of his kiss right there.

Oh, yes, that was what she'd wanted. And now that she'd
had it, she knew it wasn't enough. She wanted—needed—
more.

Just for a second, Jake was forced to wonder if he'd moved
too fast. With her hand pressed tight to her mouth, fingers
close against those soft, yielding lips, she looked startled,
taken aback. Her wide ebony eyes were huge and dark above
her concealing hand, and he couldn't tell whether the look
she turned on him was of shock or delight.

But then, slowly, she lowered that concealing hand, and
he watched in amazement as the soft, reddened lips curled

slowly and irresistibly up at the corners, turning into a wide, contented smile.

'Nicer,' she almost purred, reminding him of a small black cat that had just had its first taste of cream. 'But what I had in mind was more along the lines of this...'

Taking his face in both her hands, the soft warmth of her fingers lying along the line of his jaw, their tips resting in the beginning of his hair above his ears, she drew his face to hers, took his mouth in the softest, most sensuous, most lingering kiss he had ever known.

A kiss that blew all the fuses in his brain.

He felt as if the room had blurred around him, the lights dimming and the sounds of the street drowned by the pounding thud of his heart in his ears. And he was drowning too. Drowning in the rush of blood to his head—and other, more primitive places—in the heady aroma of her perfume, the even sexier scent of her skin. The taste of her was more intoxicating than the finest champagne, and the heavy, demanding pulse of passion set up between his legs, heating and hardening him in a second.

It was almost an agony of deprivation when she stopped, drew back, looking him straight in the face.

'Yes?' she questioned deeply.

And Jake felt that he could really only sigh his response.

*Oh, yes,* he thought privately. Hell, yes.

But outwardly he still managed to control his reactions enough to smile into her face and appear to be considering.

'Nice,' he said carefully, deliberately echoing her own response of moments earlier. 'But what *I* had in mind was more along these lines...'

Reaching for her, he clasped his hands around the bare arms exposed by the shoestring straps that supported her dress. Half lifting her from her chair, half dragging her towards him, he brought his mouth to hers in a fiercely passionate kiss. So fierce that he heard the breath leave her in a gasp of astonished response. But a moment later she had recovered and was kissing him back, enthusiastically, willingly, openly.

Urgently.

Passionately.

It was as if he had set a match to drought-dry brushwood and now he could only stand back and watch the flames lick hungrily at the perfect kindling, swelling, growing, impossible to stop as they headed towards the violent conflagration that would engulf everything in a matter of seconds.

He'd never felt anything like it. Never known a woman to respond in this way—never known *himself* to respond like this to any woman. If he had felt as if he were almost drowning just moments before, now he was very definitely going down for the third time—and enjoying every second of it.

'Mercedes...' he gasped in a much-needed second to snatch breath. 'Lady...'

But that was all he managed. And Mercedes gave him no response. No verbal response anyway. But the force of her kiss, the pressure of her hunger took his mouth again and with it any feeble attempt at coherent thought.

He was holding her shoulders even tighter, pulling her up and out of her chair, trying to close his arms around her. But the damn table was between them.

Even as he cursed the constraints forced on them by the barrier of wood and cloth and glass and china, Mercedes took action to deal with it.

A tiny twist of her shoulders, a movement upright, a couple of steps...and suddenly she was there, beside him, standing when he was still seated at the table, reaching for him blind-eyed with hunger, her mouth already taking his again.

'Jake...' she muttered against his lips. 'Oh, Jake—this is so much more than *nice*!'

She kissed him, over and over, this time greedy, snatching kisses pressed to his mouth again and again, and, blind to anything but sensation, he pulled her closer, opening his legs so that she stood between his thighs, leaning forward, her breasts crushed against his chest, her mouth locked with his.

Her hands slipped upwards to tangle in his hair, hold him tight as she kissed him again. The curve of her hips, her waist, was a carnal temptation, begging for his touch, and unable to bear it any longer, he pushed himself to his feet so that at least they were level with each other, eye to eye... But instead of making him feel easier, it only made things so much worse.

The lower part of her body was now so close to the swell of his erection, straining against the restraint of his trousers as she still stood between his thighs, that every tiny movement was sheer sensual torment. When she shifted slightly, it was like a caress that made him ache with need. If she leaned closer it set up a sweet, agonising pressure that drove a groan of response from his lips. He thought that he would burst, that his senses would explode—that he would lose consciousness with the intensity of the wild pleasure-pain.

And he knew then that he didn't care about her background, or her father, or the trouble she might bring with her, or anything. Just so long as he could have this woman—know her, kiss her—take her to his bed. He would pay any price, take any risk...

He *had* to have her.

'Upstairs,' he muttered roughly against her still-yearning mouth.

'Mmm...yes...'

It was all that Mercedes could manage; the only sounds that would leave her mouth.

She couldn't think beyond that one single word—that yes—yes—*yes* that was a pounding refrain, a scream of delight inside her fevered brain.

Her body was on fire, her thoughts melting in the heat of her blood. Jake's hands were on her breasts, cupping them through the fine material of her dress, his thumbs smoothing over the already tingling nipples, making her shudder in uncontrolled response.

'Yes…' she muttered again, against his lips this time, not wanting to take her mouth away from his even for the few tiny seconds that it took to speak.

She didn't think that she could walk; her legs felt as if they had turned to cotton wool beneath her. But Jake seemed to sense her sudden weakness and he swung her up into his arms, kicking her chair out of his way as he headed for the stairs.

The brief journey was done blind, Jake's mouth still snatching greedy, demanding kisses as he made his way, sure-footed as a cat, up the stairs, across the landing, into what she had to assume was his bedroom. Passion still blurred her eyes so that she took in nothing of her surroundings as they came down onto the bed together, him on top of her, his weight crushing her down into the yielding depths of the duvet.

'Lady, you are amazing…' he muttered against her cheek, kissing his way roughly down her face, along the arched, smooth line of her throat, across the exposed skin of her shoulder at the same time as he wrenched his shirt buttons from their fastenings, shrugging himself out of the garment and tossing it aside. 'Do you know what you do to me?'

Her only possible response was a gasp of shaken laughter as he moved, coming to lie between her legs, and there was no way she could deny the knowledge of the effect she had on him. It was there, in the heat and hardness of his body, crushed against the cradle of her pelvis, announcing the primitive hunger that had him in its grip.

His hands were urgent at the hem of her dress, twisting in the pink material, tugging it roughly upwards, exposing the lacy-topped stockings that he must have sensed by touch

alone, because his questing fingers stilled suddenly as they
met the softness of exposed flesh.

'I'd've bet on it,' he muttered, his voice shaking with unexpected laughter as he turned his head to take her mouth
once more in a fierce, passionate kiss.

But the kiss didn't linger long. Once more his demanding
mouth made the journey over her skin, and this time when
it reached the curve of her shoulder she felt the sharpness of
his teeth close over the pink strap of her dress, tugging at it
until the small bow that fastened it fell apart. The loose bodice drifted down over her breast and his mouth followed it,
kissing, licking, even occasionally grazing the soft skin with
his teeth.

And all the time those knowing hands were moving higher
under the wrenched-up skirt, sliding under the elastic at the
sides of her knickers, making her writhe in uncontrolled response. But she missed the moment when strong fingers
tugged at the waist of the sliver of silk, pulling it away and
down over her hips. because that was the same second that
his hot, hungry mouth closed over the straining tip of her
exposed breast, suckling hard and sending stinging sensations
of ecstasy racing through her.

'Oh, *Dios mio*!' The cry escaped her, soaring into the
night-darkened room, all hope of control wrenched from her.
'Jake, *amante*, Jake, *querido*—Jake, I want you now!'

In her delirium, she muttered the words in her native
Spanish, but it was clear that he caught them and translated
them quite easily. It was not lack of understanding that stilled
him suddenly, his head lifting, glazed blue eyes looking
down on her passion-flushed face.

'And I want you, my lovely—but let's not be foolish.
There are—precautions we need to take.'

Precautions?

For a moment, the word meant nothing to her, but then
realisation dawned and she nodded her head sharply, the

movement rough and urgent as the pulse that thudded through her.

'Yes—yes—do you have…'

'I do.'

Jake glanced to the side then paused, swore savagely under his breath, his long body tensing, becoming taut above her.

The slash of colour over his broad cheekbones darkened and his mouth clamped tight in an expression of disappointment that communicated itself to Mercedes.

'Jake?' Her voice had little strength in it. 'Don't say—please…'

'No.'

He shook his dark head fiercely, the movement as rough as his voice.

'No, I'm not saying I don't have any—but they're not here…They're…'

His voice trailing off, he jackknifed off the bed, pausing briefly to drop a kiss onto her heated forehead, another onto the breast his hungry hands and mouth had exposed.

'Jake…' she protested shakily, already feeling cold and disturbingly lost without the heavy, warm pressure of his body.

The heady, intoxicating excitement was ebbing away fast, leaving her feeling chilled and shivering—and desperately unsure.

'I won't be a moment, sweetheart.'

Once more his lips pressed against the smooth skin of her breast, but somehow this time their heat only served to make her realise just how cold and exposed the unkissed areas felt.

'Hold that thought, sweetheart—I'll be back.'

He didn't hesitate, didn't look back as he left the room and Mercedes could only watch him go. She opened her mouth once to call him back, to beg him not to leave her like this, not even for a second, but her voice failed her completely and not even the tiniest, most pathetic squeak came out.

She didn't want him to go—didn't want him to walk out the door, because as he went it seemed that a cold draught of reality came sneaking into the room, chilling her body and lowering her spirits as it did so.

What *was* she doing?

What sort of madness had overtaken her?

How had she come to be here, like this—with a man she hardly knew?

And then, from the back of her mind, where she knew she had pushed it in the middle of the wildness—the insanity that had gripped her from the moment that Jake had kissed her— came a memory that had her jolting upright, suddenly shivering in shock.

'Promise me something…'

It was a beloved voice that sounded inside her head. A voice that she had not heard in reality for years but the memory of which echoed like a long-loved song in her thoughts— her mother's voice.

'Promise me, darling, that you will only ever sleep with a man that you love. Promise me that you won't throw your virginity away on someone who wouldn't value it.'

What *was* she doing? Why was she lying here—waiting for a man who didn't love her, didn't even *know* her, to come back and…?

She couldn't even finish the thought. A wave of panic pushed her upwards, jumping off the bed in a rush, dashing to the door.

Jake was somewhere down the corridor, she could hear him opening a cupboard. Not taking time to think or even breathe, she crept down the stairs as fast as she could, silent in her bare feet, pulling her dress up at the bodice and down at the skirt as she did so.

Her shoes had fallen off in the hall on the way upstairs. It was the work of a second to push her feet into them; another moment to dash into the living room and snatch up her bag.

It was only then that she realised that under the slip of a dress she was naked. The knickers that Jake had removed so hungrily just a short time before were still on the bedroom floor somewhere. But they would just have to stay there; there was no way she was going back for them. Above her she could hear Jake's heavy footsteps heading back along the landing, towards the bedroom.

She just had time.

As she wrenched the front door open she heard the sudden exclamation from upstairs.

'What the—? Mercedes? Mercedes; where are—?'

The end of the shouted question was cut off as the door slammed shut behind her.

Breathing deeply in her panic, not daring to look behind her in case she should see him appear on the doorstep, or even coming after her, she broke into a desperate run and fled, not slowing until she was a long way away, out of sight and out of breath.

# CHAPTER FOUR

THE letter was lying on the mat when Jake arrived home at the end of a long, infuriating day.

So long and so infuriating a day that he walked straight over the envelope, crushing its cream-coloured elegance underfoot before he even realised that it was there. It was only when he heard the rustle of paper that he looked down and realised what it was.

'Oh, damnation!'

Something else to add to his already vicious mood. All he really wanted was a large drink and hot shower—and he didn't care in what order. But he supposed he'd better look at the damn thing now that he'd spotted it.

'Who...?'

Snatching up the missive, he turned it over, glanced at the address, and the unfamiliar stamp, and swore again, more loudly this time.

A letter from Spain was the last thing he needed right now.

A letter from Spain that made him think of Mercedes bloody Alcolar and her arrogant, manipulative family.

Apart from Ramón, of course. And his cousin would be the one who would have sent the letter.

But he wasn't even in the mood for a letter from Ramón. That hot shower was calling to him, and he needed to wash the memory of the day away.

'Sorry, mate—maybe later.'

Tossing the envelope onto the table in the hall, he headed upstairs to the bathroom, tugging his tie free at his neck as he went.

It didn't work.

In spite of the fact that he stood under the blistering, pounding water for long minutes, letting it beat down hard on his head and shoulders, drumming into his skull, nothing erased the annoyance of the day and the final humiliating insult that had driven him back home in such a rage. If anything, it made it worse, giving him time to stand and think and remember, until his teeth were clenched so tight his jaw ached, and his silent seething made his blood boil hotter than the shower.

It wasn't just today that had driven him to this. It had all started from the moment that he had been fool enough to let Mercedes Alcolar get under his skin.

Snapping the shower off, he emerged from the *en suite* bathroom into the space of his bedroom, and immediately the memories returned to engulf him, making him grit his teeth even harder.

He could almost see her. He could have sworn that he could smell her perfume on the air, as it had been on the cover of the pillows—when he'd finally got to bed the night before.

To bed, but not to sleep.

'Oh, damn her! Damn her to hell. If I could get my hands on her…'

He had thought that he had been going crazy—stark raving mad—in the moment that he had come back into the bedroom after the hasty, and infuriatingly difficult, search for the box of condoms that had not been in the first place he had looked for them—or the second.

When he had left the room, Mercedes had been lying on his bed, her long hair splayed out on the pillow behind her dark head, her slender limbs spread across the navy duvet. She had looked wantonly dishevelled with her dress pulled down to expose her breasts, the tiny skirt pushed so high it had just about disappeared. Her luscious mouth had been

swollen from his kisses, her face flushed and her eyes glazed
with passion.

He had had no thought other than that she would wait
there. That she was as hungry for him as he was for her. That
her body ached in need as much as his did.

Not being able to find what he was looking for had only
added to his frustration. He had wrenched open drawers,
hunting through them roughly, leaving things in disarray.
And when he had spotted the small package he had pounced
on it on a wave of relief.

He didn't think he'd been away long. The walk back
across the landing had only taken seconds, he was sure of it.
And yet, when he had pushed open the door, he had known
instantly that something was wrong.

It was the silence that had got to him first. The silence and
the intense stillness of the room—the sense of emptiness.

He had stopped dead in the doorway, staring at the vacant
bed, unable to believe his eyes.

'What the—?'

The words had been wrenched from him in shock and in-
credulity.

'*Mercedes?* Mercedes, where are you?'

The sound of a door downstairs slamming had cut into his
words, startling him. But even then he hadn't connected it
with her disappearance.

Like a fool, like a total, blind idiot, he had thought that
she must still be there. He had even checked in the bathroom,
yanking open the door to the *en suite*, and glaring in, fully
expecting to find her washing her face or some such thing.

'Mercedes, what the hell…?'

But that room had been empty too and it had been only
then that he had connected the sound of the door banging
shut downstairs with the suddenly silent rooms.

He had thought it would be an easy matter to go after her,
catch her up, demand an explanation. But he had found no

sign of her. She had vanished into the night like some modern-day Cinderella, not even leaving behind her a reminder in the shape of a single shoe.

But she had left something much more intimate, Jake remembered, zipping up an elderly pair of jeans, his eyes going to the small bundle of pale blue silk that still lay on the top of a walnut chest of drawers.

The knickers that Mercedes had been wearing yesterday night. And that she had left behind in her haste to escape.

He allowed himself a small, grim smile of dark satisfaction as he pulled on a black tee shirt, and tucked it in at his narrow waist.

One day he was going to meet up with Mercedes Alcolar again, and when he did that tiny piece of feminine clothing was going to be his major weapon in the revenge he planned to take on her.

Revenge.

The word reverberated inside his head as he went back downstairs, still thinking longingly of that drink.

He had never actually thought of himself as a vengeful man, and yesterday, when he had found the slip of silk lying on the rich, darker blue of the carpet, no such thought had come into his head. In fact his first thought, on discovering that she had run out on him, had been concern.

'More fool, you!' he muttered to himself, pouring a generous amount of Scotch into a glass. 'Thinking she might have been upset! Huh!'

He'd hunted for her for some time, even calling her name, but in the end had had to admit defeat and head back to the house, where he'd been about to find her friend Antonia's phone number when he'd been interrupted by an unwelcome arrival.

At first, when he'd heard the key in the door, he'd thought it was Mercedes back again, only recalling a moment later that she didn't possess a key. The person who had had one, though, was Karen Maitland, the woman who, up until a week ago, had been his girlfriend.

And the woman who, in spite of his declaration to the contrary, had still thought that she was. He'd asked for the key back but she must have had it copied. And there she had been, walking into his home as if she still had every right to be there.

'Jake!' she had called as soon as she'd opened the door. 'Darling—I'm back. I got away early so I came straight round to see you. I need your loving so badly. Have you missed me, lover?'

Jake grimaced at that particular memory, taking a long swallow of his drink and throwing himself down into a chair, staring broodingly at the empty fireplace. Karen had always been a particularly clinging sort of character, and when he had decided to end their relationship, a relationship that had been going nowhere for some time, he had braced himself for every sort of a scene, for tears, sobs, protests, and he had been frankly surprised when they hadn't materialised. Instead he'd believed that she had accepted the inevitable with a good grace.

Last night he had been forced to accept that he'd been wrong.

Last night, he had had to put up with the storms and tantrums that he had anticipated the first time. And last night he had not been in any mood to play the nice guy, or even attempt to appease her in the slightest.

His body had been in an agony of frustration at the abrupt and unexpected ending to the long night of lovemaking he had been looking forward to. He'd ached all over, his mind still whirling in confusion, wondering just what had happened in the few moments that he had been out of the bedroom, leaving Mercedes alone. And with his thoughts and senses preoccupied with one woman, he hadn't found it easy to turn his attention to the petulant demands and hysterical scene created by another.

He'd given her short shrift. He'd told her bluntly that they were finished and demanded his key back. Which had only resulted in more tears.

By the time he'd got her back out the door—*without* the key—all he'd been able to think of was getting to the phone and ringing Antonia's flat.

'Is Mercedes there?' he demanded as soon as the receiver was picked up, not waiting for her to speak.

'She—who's that?' A sudden suspicion crept into the voice at the other end of the line.

'It's Jake Taverner.'

Even as he spoke he could hear the whispered conversation in Antonia's flat, not quite muffled by a hastily concealing hand.

'Tell Mercedes I want to talk to her!' he snapped, all the concern evaporating in a rush at this evidence that she was obviously there and safe. The space left behind was just as rapidly refilled with a flood of anger and frustration at the way she had behaved.

'She doesn't want to speak to you.'

'Antonia, or whatever your name is—' Jake's voice was dangerous, hissing out between the teeth he had clenched against the temper that was fraying wildly at the edges '—tell her to come to the damn phone!'

'She doesn't want to speak to you!'

Couldn't the girl say anything else?

'Tell her—'

But he never managed to finish the sentence. Halfway through, the phone was slammed down at the other end, cutting him off.

And when he tried redialling, all he got was the engaged tone ringing on and on and on. The phone was off the hook.

He'd been every sort of a fool!

Jake brought his free hand down on the arm of his chair now with a heavy thud, his clenched fist and whitened knuckles revealing the force of his mood.

Even then, he'd not realised quite how much he'd been taken for a ride. *That* had been brought home to him by the response he'd had this evening—when he'd gone round to Antonia's flat in an attempt to speak to Mercedes.

A vain attempt.

She'd been there of course. He hadn't seen her, but her friend hadn't even tried to hide the fact that Mercedes was somewhere behind her, out of sight, hidden by the barely open door. Jake could just imagine her standing there, listening to the conversation, probably smiling to herself as she heard Antonia give him the brush-off, the smile growing wider as her friend delivered the killer blow.

'She wants me to say that from your reputation as a stud, she was hoping for something better. Quite frankly you didn't even match up to what she already has, so she didn't want to waste any more of her time bothering with you.'

*She didn't want to waste any more of her time bothering with you.*

Jake tossed the last of the whisky to the back of his throat and swallowed hard, closing his eyes briefly against the burn of the spirit.

He'd been every sort of a damn fool!

In all of this, the one thing that he had never considered, the one thing that had never crossed his mind, was that Mercedes might have been using him. He had been so knocked off balance by just the sight of her, and his own overwhelming physical response to her, that he had never stopped to consider that she might not feel the same. In fact, he had taken her behaviour to indicate that she did.

Now he was looking back at it through very different eyes. Through eyes turned cold and analytical by hindsight. And that hindsight, especially when taken together with the mem-

ory of the cold, haughty look she had turned on him in the
very first moment she had ever seen him, put a very different
interpretation on events.

Mercedes Alcolar was a tease. A damn selfish, provocative, shameless, wanton tormentor. She thought nothing of
setting herself to turn a man on—and he *had* been so turned
on that even now he still burned with the hungry, gnawing
ache of bitter frustration—and then leaving him flat.

Very bloody flat.

Totally, sickeningly, agonisingly flat.

But the problem was that, underneath the feeling of being
totally let down, used, and then dropped as if from a great
height, the heat of the fires she had lit in his soul still burned.
He hated her and yet he couldn't hate her enough to never
want to see her again.

He detested the games she had played and yet he would
have given anything to have her right back here, playing
them with him all over again.

He loathed the person she was, the rotten reality behind
the beauty of the high cheekbones, the smooth olive skin, the
lustrous hair and eyes; and yet he knew that if she were to
appear here, in this room, right now, he would fall under the
spell of that beauty at once, and not even try to fight against
it.

'Hellfire!'

He needed another drink.

He needed more than one.

What he really needed was to get totally, abjectly, blindly
drunk—so drunk that he couldn't remember his own name,
let alone that of Mercedes Alcolar. And maybe another drink
would wipe his mind clean, blotting out the hatefully erotic
image of her as he had last seen her, lying splayed out on
his bed, half naked, abandoned, warm and apparently welcoming, seeming to want him as much as he wanted her.

An image that he now knew to be nothing but a lie.

The whisky bottle was empty and he headed towards the kitchen for a replacement. To get there, he had to cross the hall, and he noticed once more the long, cream-coloured envelope he had discarded on the table there.

He might as well see what Ramón had to say.

The letter he was expecting wasn't inside the envelope. Instead, there was a beautifully printed card, sent from someone Jake had never heard of.

'Who the devil is Alfredo Medrano?'

His eyes skimmed the elegant script quickly, stopped dead in astonishment, and then went back more slowly, to read it over again.

'Daughter Estrella—marriage to Ramón Dario…'

Ramón was getting married! There had been no word of this the last time he had seen his cousin. But then, he had to admit, he hadn't spoken to Ramón for several months, never mind spent time with him.

And now, out of the blue, Ramón was getting married to a woman called Estrella Medrano, someone who hadn't even been in the picture the last time they had met. If she had, then Ramón would have talked of her.

Jake was about to drop the invitation back onto the table, when a sudden thought struck him and had him standing still, tapping the side of the envelope over and over on the back of his hand as he thought this through.

Ramón was getting married. It would be a family wedding—an *Alcolar* family wedding. Because of the undisguised ill-feeling between his aunt's family and that of the man who had turned out to be his father, Ramón had always kept the two sides of his family totally separate—so that now, as a result, no one would be expecting Ramón's unknown cousin to turn up.

Least of all the only Alcolar daughter.

A grim smile curled his mouth up at the corners, grew into a wicked grin of fiendish satisfaction.

It seemed that he and Mercedes Alcolar were destined to meet again far sooner than he had anticipated—and this time the advantage would be all on his side.

# CHAPTER FIVE

FOR a day that had started out so well and so happily, her half-brother's wedding was turning into the event from hell, Mercedes told herself as she tried once more to manoeuvre her way across the huge, elegant ballroom where the reception was being held, without being spotted by one particular man.

The last man on earth she had expected to see at this particular event.

The last man on earth she had wanted to see *anywhere*, ever again.

And just when she had thought that she was actually starting to put the memory of the events in London right behind her.

She had had such fun helping her about-to-be-brand-new sister-in-law get ready for the wedding, only leaving at the very last minute because Estrella had insisted that no one, but no one, saw her dress until she reached the church.

The dress had caused a sensation, both in the church and later, when no one had been able to stop talking about it. But by then Mercedes had been past caring, mentally bludgeoned into a state of dazed horror by the shock of realising that Jake Taverner was here, amongst the wedding guests, in the congregation in the church. The sight of him had been like the thud of an arrow into her heart, tearing its way through sensitive, unaware flesh and ripping open the misery of humiliating memories she didn't want to recall.

'Why so interested in the Englishman, little sister?' Her brother Alex's voice interrupted her unhappy thoughts, a grin curving his mouth and revealing teeth white against the tanned skin of his face. 'Don't tell me you—'

'No!' Mercedes burst out before Alex could take the question to its inevitable conclusion and ask if she was interested in the Englishman—as a man.

But the question made her painfully aware of the way that she had been staring from the safety of the space behind the broad pillar at this side of the crowded ballroom and she felt once again the lurching panic that had assailed her in the moment that she had arrived at the church and seen Jake Taverner for the first time.

He had been standing in the churchyard, talking to Ramón, and laughing openly at something her brother had been saying. His dark head had been thrown back, eyes half closed, and his deep brown hair had been gleaming in the warmth of the afternoon sun.

'No, of course not,' she continued more softly, painfully aware of the way that the sharpness of her tone, the speed of her response, had risked giving too much away.

She didn't want anyone to know how she was feeling, not even her adored older brother, the one closest to her in age of the three sons of Juan Alcolar.

'I—I was just wondering who he was because he sort of stuck out—an Englishman at a Spanish family wedding. I—wasn't expecting it.'

That much at least was the exact truth. If she had to pick one person she least wanted to see—one she prayed would never come into her life again, let alone appear at this, a major social event of the year, and a very special, very happy family occasion—then the name Jake Taverner would have been the first to spring into her mind. But of course she would never have thought—never have *dreamed*—that he was in the least likely to reappear in her world, let alone here and now, hundreds of miles and several weeks from the date and the place where they had first met.

A meeting she had tried, again and again, to put out of her mind, but never succeeded. The memory of it shadowed her days, haunted her nights, and try as she might she just couldn't push it from her thoughts.

'He's a friend of Ramón's,' Alex continued, and Mercedes had to pray that she hadn't missed anything important in the moments when memory and reluctant recall had blurred her thoughts, sending them back several weeks to the time she had spent in England. 'Some media mogul in the UK. Did you want to be introduced?'

'No, thanks.'

She couldn't erase the rough emphasis of real feeling from her voice. She could just imagine the scenario—Alex saying to Jake, 'I'd like you to meet my sister.' The look on the other man's face would be a picture.

Not for the first time, she had cause to be thankful for her family's complicated background, so that only she and Joaquin, her eldest and only full brother, actually bore her father's name. Clearly, in London, Jake Taverner hadn't connected Mercedes Alcolar with Ramón Dario, the man who now turned out to be his friend. And of course she had never suspected that her middle brother knew anything about the man she had privately nicknamed *El Diablo*—the devil.

Because, like the devil in the Garden of Eden, he had come into her life and taken away her innocence as surely as if he had made love to her that night. Mercedes' skin crawled at the recollection of her abandoned, wild behaviour, the sudden terrifying panic—and, even worse, the aftermath.

Because she had been fool enough to go back.

When the panic that had gripped her had eventually died down, and a whole new sense of reality had taken its place, she had suddenly felt a complete fool for running like that. She hadn't needed to escape. Jake wasn't a monster. Surely if she had explained, he would have understood—he wouldn't have forced her. She should at least have given him a chance.

And so she had gone back; making her way through the night-dark streets until she had come within a hundred metres or so of his house. But that was when she had seen the taxi arrive. The black cab had pulled up outside his door, and a tall, willowy woman with stunning short-cropped platinum-blonde hair had got out, carrying a small suitcase.

As Mercedes had watched, she had taken a key from her bag and pushed it into the lock.

And as the door had opened she had called out in a voice that had carried down the silent street.

'Jake! Darling—I'm back. I got away early so I came straight round to see you. I need your loving so badly. Have you missed me, lover?'

She'd run properly then. She'd turned and fled as if all the devils in hell were after her. For the first time, luck had been on her side and she'd been able to flag down a taxi only moments later. She'd managed to get home before she was physically sick, her stomach heaving violently at the way that she had been caught.

Jake had moved in on her, cynically and callously, using her as a passing distraction, a one-night stand, to fill the boredom and frustration of the time while his girlfriend was away. And she'd fallen straight into his arms like the naïve, stupid idiot she was. She could only be grateful that she'd got out of there in time, thanking her mother's memory for the timely warning.

She had hoped that the passage of time might help to push the thoughts of that night from her mind. That with each day that passed the recollection would blur, eventually growing dim, fading completely from her mind. All she had to do was to keep busy and not to *think*.

And keeping busy had, at least, been easy. The preparations for Ramón's sudden and totally unexpected wedding had involved the whole family in a flurry of activity that had taken up so much time and concentration that it had been impossible to think of anything else.

Until she had arrived at the wedding today, and had seen him and felt her legs weaken beneath her, her brain fog with panic until it felt as if her head were stuffed with cotton wool.

If she could have done she would have turned right round and walked away, as far and as fast as she could. But how could she not attend her brother's wedding? Or the reception afterwards? She could only pray that he wouldn't spot her in the crowded, noisy room. Or that he would leave early and she would be spared having to come face to face with him.

So far she had managed quite well. But now Ramón and Estrella were departing, leaving to start on their honeymoon, and she would be expected to go out to wave them off. She would have to join the smaller crowd in the courtyard…

Perhaps he wouldn't see her.

Perhaps she would get away with hiding at the edge of the laughing, cheering crowd, and not letting herself be visible to the keen, probing, ice-blue eyes that she knew were concealed under those heavy, shadowed lids.

And at first it seemed that her luck had held out. She couldn't spot Jake Taverner as she made her way down the long, curving staircase of the Castillo Medrano. He was nowhere in sight as the sleek black limousine pulled up outside the heavy panelled wooden doors and the chauffeur jumped out, opening the car so that Ramón and his bride could get in.

But that was where her luck failed her. Because of course Estrella, who in the past few weeks had come to see her as a friend and an ally, almost as a sister, wouldn't leave at once, hesitating, and looking round her.

'Mercedes!' she called, beckoning the other girl to her, unaware of the total horror of embarrassment that her shout and her gesture had opened up inside Mercedes' mind. 'Let me give you a hug before I go.'

She wouldn't take no for an answer. And anyway, it was already way too late. Singled out, and with almost all eyes turning in her direction, Mercedes knew that she had no option but to move forward and be enfolded in a warm, perfumed embrace. And then Ramón too hugged her hard and affectionately, though it was obvious his thoughts were elsewhere, presumably on the honeymoon ahead of him.

'Goodbye, little sister. Be good while I'm away.'

And then he was gone, sliding into the car beside his new wife and slamming the door, leaving Mercedes standing alone, and totally exposed in the wide, sunny space of the courtyard.

And that was when she looked up and saw him again. Saw him standing across the courtyard, leaning against the wall, strong arms folded across his chest as they had been the very first time she had ever seen him, at that party in London.

And just as he had been then, so he was watching her now, blue, blue eyes intent on her face.

Her heart skipped, stood still for a long, terrible moment, then started beating again, in double-quick time. But that moment had been long enough for the rest of her family to gather round her. The tall frame of her oldest brother Joaquin, his arm around his pregnant wife, came between her and the cold-eyed scrutiny. Alex, his wife Louise, and their baby daughter huddled close. Even her father, a man not given to emotional displays or words, joined them to wave after the departing car, and when she looked again Jake Taverner was gone.

Relief was like the splash of icy water in her face, so great that she actually sagged against her father's side, resting her hand on the strength of his arm to support herself.

Perhaps he *hadn't* recognised her. After all, she'd probably be fooling herself that she was so memorable to a man like Jake Taverner.

Or perhaps the vicious-tongued message that Tonia had taken it on herself to make up and throw at him had had the desired effect and driven him away from her for good.

'She wants me to say that from your reputation as a stud, she was hoping for something better. Quite frankly you didn't even match up to what she already has, so she didn't want to waste any more of her time bothering with you.'

Perhaps she'd actually got away with it.

'Mercedes...'

The voice from behind her froze her movement in an instant, bringing her to an abrupt halt in the tiled and panelled hall.

Only one man used her name in just that way. One man used the native Spanish pronunciation, but with the faint touch of an English accent to create a sound that was burned into her memories in notes of fire.

'Mercedes.'

Oh, no! Dear God, please, *no*!


He spotted her from the moment she walked into the church.

How could he not, Jake Taverner asked himself, when that slight, elegant figure was etched into his memories, lingering in his thoughts for weeks? He hadn't been able to get her out of his mind ever since. But what he hadn't expected was the sheer physical force with which her appearance affected him; the sensation almost like a blow that rocked him back in the carved wooden pew where he, like everyone else, was sitting, waiting for the arrival of his cousin's bride.

He didn't know which emotion had the most effect on him. The gut-twisting impact of the aching physical need that made his thoughts reel, or the slow burn of cold, dark anger that swirled like a dangerous undercurrent, threatening to overwhelm all other feelings.

The physical desire slammed into him as he watched her walk down the aisle, her slender frame poured into a neat, tailored sky-blue summer suit, long legs in silky stockings visible below the barely knee-length skirt. The high heels of her shoes tapped on the stone paving of the floor of the church and he could have sworn that he caught a faint waft of her perfume as she passed him, totally unaware of his presence. Her shining hair gleamed blue-black as it fell in a smooth, sleek style around the oval face, and, although he couldn't see them from here, he knew that her eyes were brown, dark as rich chocolate, and every bit as tempting.

'*Sì*... That's right. My name is Mercedes Alcolar...'

The echo of her voice sounded in his mind, taking him back to the moment that he had introduced himself to her. And the soft, enticing sound of the words, enhanced by the lilting effect of her hesitant Spanish accent, had reached out and coiled around him, twisting in his senses and holding him prisoner in an instant.

He hadn't been able to think of anything beyond taking this woman to bed. In his imagination he had already been stripping the clothes from her body and feeling the warm velvet of her skin under his hands, tasting it with his mouth. And those same thoughts assailed him again now, appallingly inappropriate to the place he was in, the atmosphere of the wedding.

But then he noticed the way that Mercedes' hand was tucked into another man's arm, her touch intimate and relaxed, her fingers resting on the dark cloth of his jacket. Her smile into his face was warm and enticing—as warm and enticing as it had once been to Jake himself—and her companion responded to it instantly, ducking his dark head to catch something she said.

Not one of her brothers, Jake noted grimly, dragging his eyes away and focusing them on the altar rails where Ramón and his two brothers stood together, awaiting the arrival of

Ramón's bride. Not one of her brothers, but he couldn't allow himself to think about just *who* the man might be or the black fury that was burning in the pit of his stomach would boil upwards, spilling out in a way that would ruin the day—and his reputation—for ever.

So he kept the flames tamped down, held them back by sheer force of will and refused to let himself glance once more in Mercedes' direction. Somehow he sat through the wedding ceremony, even the reception, though the struggle he had with his temper made it impossible to eat anything, and the wine he drank only fed the darkness of his mood, turning it blacker and more bitter by the second. He only caught a rare glimpse of Mercedes, once more with her tall, dark escort, but he forced himself to look away again fast, before his grip on his control broke completely.

He would not spoil the day for Ramón and Estrella, but when they had gone… Then he and Mercedes Alcolar would have some serious talking to do.

His chance came as the limousine that was taking the newly married pair away on holiday drove out of the *castillo* gates and disappeared from sight. At once all the guests and family who had come out to wave it off turned and headed back inside, laughing and chattering as they went.

And at the back of them, slender and seductive in her designer suit, those ridiculously high heels making her progress over the cobbled courtyard slow and awkward—and, best of all, alone this time—was the woman he had been looking for.

'Mercedes…'

At first he thought that she hadn't heard him. She kept her head turned away, the set of her shoulders like a shield against possible attack. But then he saw that her determined steps had faltered just a little, that her pace was slowing.

'Mercedes,' he said again, and, striding forward, he caught hold of her arm, restraining her.

She stopped, whirled, gasped. Just for a moment her dark eyes opened wide and something wild flared in them, but almost immediately she had stilled again, and a careful, controlled mask came down over her fine-boned features.

In an instant she was another woman; one a million light-years away from the woman he had taken to his bed.

That woman had been all fire and heat, brilliant as a summer lightning storm. This one was pure ice through and through. From her motionless, tautly held body to her stiff, expressionless face and those cold, cold eyes that stared into his.

This woman was the cold-eyed, arrogant bitch who had turned a look of ice on him from across a room.

'Do I know you?' she managed, obviously forcing the words from lips that barely opened, they were held so tight. 'Have we met before?'

She was so convincing that another, weaker man might have been fooled. A less observant man too might not have seen the momentary flash of a revealing expression across her face, betraying her innermost feelings. But Jake had seen it and seen the sudden flare of something in her eyes. Something that changed the rich chocolate to a burning bronze and told him that she was every inch as aware of him as he was of her.

'Is that a serious question?' he demanded, unable to believe that she was actually trying this on.

'Perfectly serious.'

Her chin came up even more defiantly, tilting her perfect little nose higher in the air. And the cold, dark eyes met his head on, rejection the only emotion he could see in them.

'*Do* I know you?'

'You know you do.'

'I know nothing of the sort.'

She even managed a smile, though it was so false and

brittle that he almost expected it to shatter and fall as splinters onto the ground at his feet.

'I think you must be mistaken—Mr…'

Jake didn't even honour the pointed hint that he should give her his name with as much as an acknowledgement. This 'I don't remember you' act didn't convince him for one moment.

'No mistake, I assure you. You know that, and I know that—but if you need any further convincing…'

He had been thinking of just this moment when he had packed his case, and again this morning as he had dressed for the wedding. In the left-hand pocket of his suit jacket, the sliver of silk not even bulky enough to spoil the line of the superb tailoring was the evidence of the truth—the knickers she had left behind in her headlong flight that night in London.

He pulled them out, crushed in his hand, opened his fingers just enough so that she could see exactly what he held—but had no chance of reaching for them, trying to snatch them away from him.

The effect was everything he had hoped for.

Her breath escaped in a gasp of shock; all the colour fled from her cheeks so that her red-lipsticked mouth looked garish and wild in contrast to the pale olive skin.

She had opened her mouth to say something, then closed it again, swallowing violently. She was about to try again when a tall, dark, male figure appeared in the doorway, obviously looking for her.

'Mercedes, are you coming in? We're waiting…'

Of course. Jake clamped his jaw tight shut on the anger that almost escaped him. Juan Alcolar, the patriarch of the whole, complicated family. Rich, powerful and arrogant as hell. The man who had messed up his mother's family so badly that she had never truly recovered; so that bitter memories still darkened her life to this day. And Mercedes' father.

Like father, like daughter?

It would seem so. He'd be willing to bet on it anyway.

'Coming, *Papá*.'

She'd regained her composure, it seemed. Those dark eyes swung back to his face, still no sign of any softening deep within them.

'If you will excuse me.'

It was barely polite, her relief at being able to escape making it so plain that she was only lingering long enough to say the words. In fact she was already turning away as she spoke.

Jake watched her walk up the stone steps towards her father. Her head was high, the slender line of her back taut and straight and as unyielding as the way her father held his. She didn't spare him even a single glance back.

*Like father, like daughter.*

'No, lady,' he growled under his breath. 'You're the one who's made the mistake.'

Mercedes Alcolar was clearly her father's daughter. He would do well to remember that in the future.

And there *was* going to be a future for himself and Señorita Alcolar; he was determined on that.

For one thing she had got so far under his skin that she was like an itch that he could never scratch.

And for another, he and Señorita Mercedes Alcolar had a lot of unfinished business between them. Business that Jake had every intention of following through on.

She might think that by refusing to admit she knew him she had dodged the issue of what had happened between them in London, and that now that she'd walked away it was over and done with—but she'd be wrong.

It was finished when he said it was, and not before.

# CHAPTER SIX

IF ONLY she hadn't gone to London!

It was the thought that wouldn't leave Mercedes' head, but plagued her mind even as she returned to the reception and set herself to smiling, chatting, dancing again.

If she had stayed at home and not set foot in the English capital, her life would still be on its normal, peaceful, happy track. She would have been able to prepare for Ramón's wedding without any hesitation or distracting thoughts. And she would have been able to enjoy the day without the lurching panic that had assailed her in the moment that she had walked into the church and seen Jake Taverner sitting amongst the congregation.

What would she have felt if that had been the first time that she had seen him? If she had walked down the aisle and seen him there, never having encountered him in her life before?

Would she have experienced that stunning sensation that was like a blow to her heart at just the sight of him?

From the way that her heart thudded in response to her own inner question, she knew that the only answer was yes.

'Ouch!'

A pointed, indignant protest broke into her thoughts, making her hesitate, pause and blush with embarrassed colour as she realised that, her concentration totally shot, her thoughts elsewhere, she hadn't been dancing with her usual skill and elegance. Lost in unwanted memories, she hadn't been concentrating on what she was doing with her feet and as a result one of the high, narrow heels of her shoes had landed squarely on the toes of her partner, almost piercing his glossy leather boots.

'Oh, Miguel, I'm sorry! I just wasn't thinking!'

'That much I guessed for myself,' her partner returned, his expression wry. 'What is it, *querida*? Don't you want to dance any more?'

'I—well, no, not really,' Mercedes admitted.

She'd flown into the protection of Miguel's company as soon as she'd gone back inside the *castillo*. Surely, seeing the two of them together, Jake Taverner would believe they were partners for more than the dance, and keep his distance.

'I think I've had a little too much champagne.'

'Well, that's the whole point of a wedding—to celebrate. But maybe you'd benefit from some fresh air. We could go into the garden.'

'It is incredibly hot in here.'

She knew that Miguel had an ulterior motive for wanting to get her into the garden—alone with him. But, frankly, she didn't care. In fact, it could quite possibly be the best thing. A way of distracting herself from Jake Taverner's disturbing presence, and the knowledge of the way those blue eyes were watching her, following every move she made, everything she did.

And maybe, if she was lucky, Miguel's kisses might be just what she needed. They might make her realise that what had happened in London had just been a mental aberration. That she had just been dreaming about the effect Jake had had on her. That it hadn't been as devastating as she remembered, but simply a combination of her hormones, the setting, the excitement of being in England—and a little too much to drink.

'Then come with me.'

Miguel's arm came round her, clutching rather too tightly, holding her a little too close. But Mercedes decided not to let it worry her. She didn't try to move away. Instead, she let herself cuddle even closer, resting her head against Miguel's shoulder, smiling up at him deliberately.

Let Jake make what he wanted of that! If he thought that she was not on her own, that she had another man who was interested in her—more than interested—then surely he would give up on his attempt to rake over their meeting in London and let it go, leaving her in peace?

So she concentrated all her attention on Miguel, gazing into his eyes like the most besotted lover ever as she let him lead her away from the ballroom and towards the huge French doors that opened out into the garden beyond. She wouldn't look, wouldn't even risk a tiny glance to see Jake's reaction, though every nerve in her body was tight, tense, on red alert. She couldn't see him, but she knew that somewhere, in some other part of the room, he was watching her and would draw his own conclusions.

'Who's that that the Alcolar daughter is with?' Jake asked the man he had been chatting to—pretending to chat to—for the last ten minutes. He had really been fully occupied watching Mercedes dance, unable to take his eyes off the lithe, sinuously sexy movements of her body, the way her hips swayed instinctively to the rhythm.

'Do you mean Miguel? Miguel Hernandez?'

The other man glanced in the direction Jake was looking and nodded slowly.

'Yes, that's Miguel. It'll be their wedding next, the gossips say.'

'They're *engaged*?'

Jake couldn't keep the shock from his voice, but he managed to suppress some of the disgust that might give away exactly how he was feeling.

She had been such a tease with him, had behaved so wantonly—and she was engaged to be married to someone else?

'Oh, I don't think it's official quite yet. But according to my wife it's on the cards—at least if Papá Alcolar and young Hernandez' father have their say. They've been actively encouraging this union—though it doesn't look as if the young ones are exactly opposed to the idea.'

It certainly didn't, Jake reflected as the man excused himself and moved away. And that gave him a possible explanation for the way that Mercedes had behaved—she was terrified of what he might reveal about her.

She might not remember—correction—she might *claim* not to remember him, but he remembered her only too well, Jake growled to himself as he watched Mercedes cross the room, lovingly draped all over the young man she had been dancing with. And he remembered the way that she was behaving too.

She had been exactly that way with him from the moment he had called to pick her up to bring her to his apartment for the dinner.

She had draped herself over him as well, he recalled, his body tightening hot and hard just at the memory. She had cuddled close, the warmth of her body reaching through his clothes, the scent of her skin rising to torment his hyper-aware senses, driving him almost insane with hunger with each breath he drew in.

And she had laughed in just that way too, looking up into his eyes in that devoted, totally absorbed way as if there were no one else in the entire world but him.

And he had damn well swallowed it. Just as the poor idiot she was with now was swallowing it, hook, line and sinker. She was playing him for a fool—just as she had played Jake himself. Enticing. Inviting. Seducing. Promising so much—and yet knowing all the time that she had no intention at all of delivering.

Unless, of course, this Miguel was the one that she *would* deliver to.

'Hellfire!'

The idea struck home with such a brutal force that the stem of the glass he was holding actually snapped beneath the sudden, convulsive pressure of his hard fingers and he had to drop it hastily onto the nearest table before he ripped his hand to ribbons on the jagged spikes.

Was *that* why she had run out on him?

Had she suddenly remembered the boyfriend—the poor, gullible idiot she had on a string at home—and fled in a belated attack of much-needed conscience?

As if the thought had given him a push, he found he was moving, striding fast across the crowded dance floor, turning sharply to dodge past couples, closely entwined, totally absorbed in each other. Once or twice he had to slow, his progress impeded by the women who moved into his path, fixed their eyes on his, smiled encouragingly.

At any other time he might have been interested, might have lingered. But none of them distracted him enough to soothe the blaze of his thoughts, the rage of his mind.

Not tonight.

'Perdón, señorita...'

Automatically he dropped into the Spanish learned from many holidays spent with his mother's family; endless hours shared with his cousin Ramón.

'I have to see someone.'

He knew his voice sounded clipped and cold, his intonation curt, but his mind wasn't on the polite niceties—and definitely not on the thought of meeting, maybe dating, another woman. He hadn't had any thoughts like that since the moment he had first spotted Mercedes Alcolar across the room at a noisy, smoky media party.

Because from the moment that he had first seen her, he had been hooked, caught, entranced—trapped. She had got under his skin and he didn't think he would ever be free. *Nothing* could have stopped him then; not even the knowledge that she was the child of the man he had grown up thinking of as the Big Bad Wolf, the Wicked Giant and the Evil Magician all rolled into one could have stilled his feet. Just as nothing could stop him now.

'No way,' Jake muttered to himself. 'No way at all.'

The cooling air of the evening hit him in the face as he stepped out into the garden, making him draw in a sharp, raw breath. It had been almost as warm as this on that night that she had come to his apartment, wearing that tiny slip of a dress, pink with white spots on it, and a skirt so short it was barely decent.

'Miguel, no.'

The voice—*her* voice—came from a short distance away, in the shadows, beyond where the bright lights of the ball-room spilled out over the huge garden. Immediately Jake's head turned in the direction of the sound, his eyes searching the darkness, trying to see where she was.

'Don't be a tease.'

It was the other man—Miguel Hernandez—who spoke, and just the tone of his words set Jake's teeth on edge. They were husky, possessive, almost gloating. The sound of a man who knew he was going to get his way. A man for whom the protest was only part of the game—a touch of foreplay to build up anticipation.

And Mercedes the flirt, Mercedes the temptress, the si-ren—Mercedes the cold-blooded little tease had another man trapped, entangled in her coils...

'You know why we're here.'

'But...' there was a note of protest in her voice '...you're going to ruin my dress—this wall is rough...'

'Then that's soon remedied.'

A blur of movement just ahead made Jake pause, watch. In a moment he saw more clearly. Saw the way that Miguel, who had had his back to him, turned, bringing Mercedes with him, so that now he was leaning against the uneven stone wall, his legs spread wide to accommodate the slender body of the woman who stood between them.

'Better now?' he asked roughly, the sudden sharpening of something driving the laughter from his tone.

Jake knew only too well what *that* tone meant. The smug satisfaction in the two words was something that any male would recognise. Especially with a woman as beautiful and sexy as Mercedes standing so intimately close.

She'd done exactly the same with him, he recalled bitterly. Exactly the same. And his body heated, hardened at just the memory, making him want to groan aloud in hungry desire.

He could almost feel the pressure of her slender thighs between his; the faint friction when she moved that was an agony of delight...

A sudden sound grabbed his attention, dragging his thoughts back from the darkly erotic path down which they were wandering and forcing him unwillingly into the present.

'Kiss me!'

It was Miguel who'd spoken, still totally unaware of their audience, the silent watcher in the shadows. And the thickening of his tone suddenly set Jake's nerves on edge, brought his head up, his eyes narrowing, made him watch more closely.

Things were not quite as he had at first assumed. There was a tension in Mercedes' slender spine that he hadn't noticed at the start. And she seemed to be holding herself away from this Miguel, rather than pressing close to him as he had first thought.

'I said kiss me!'

'I have kissed you!' Mercedes protested, her tone sharpening noticeably. As he heard it, the burningly erotic feeling evaporated sharply, to be replaced by an edgy itch of antagonism, but whether at her, at Miguel, or even himself, Jake couldn't begin to tell.

'So kiss me again.'

'I'd rather go in.'

'And I'd rather stay here, with my woman.'

'I'm not your woman!'

'Oh, yes, you are.'

That possessive 'my woman' grated savagely. Was the bastard *blind*? Couldn't he see that it was the last thing she wanted to hear?

'You know our parents mean us to be together. You're mine and it's about time you started to show it.'

'Miguel, no!'

There was real panic in her voice now. But apparently the louse she was with either didn't hear it or was not taking no for an answer.

'Mercedes, yes...'

The thoughts were erased in a blaze of black fury as Jake saw Miguel's hands slide down her slender blue-clad back, caressing her hips and closing over the sweet swell of her buttocks.

'You're mine, all mine, to do with as I—'

There was a red haze before his eyes, a wild buzzing in his ears.

'No!'

The sound of his fury was like an explosion in the dark as he lurched forward, grabbing at the other man and hauling him away from Mercedes, flinging him back against the wall.

'No, damn you! No way! You leave her alone!'

'Oh, yeah?' Miguel tossed back, blinking in dazed shock that in no way reduced the aggression of his tone. 'And why the hell should I do as you say?'

Jake didn't stop to think. The words sprang from his lips without a second's hesitation, produced by nothing other than the need to silence the other man before he could speak again.

'Because she's mine!' he said, flinging the words into the dark, angry face. 'Because she's not your woman—she's mine!'

# CHAPTER SEVEN

MERCEDES had known that she was in trouble from the moment that she'd stepped outside.

The truth was that she should never have embarked on this pretence at flirting with Miguel. She knew she had only done so because she was running away from any potential confrontation with Jake Taverner. But they had barely been outside a few seconds before she had had to wonder just how much he had had to drink. Certainly there was a sheen of sweat lying over his skin and his eyes seemed to glitter far more than they had ever done before.

And now Miguel's hands were roving over her, cupping her hips and forcing her intimately nearer to him. No matter how she tried to struggle, to twist her way free from the clinging hands on her buttocks, she could barely fight against his determined strength.

'You're mine, all mine, to do with as I—'

His voice was rough and thick, his eyes glazed, his breath hot and heavy on her cheek.

*No!*

The rejection sounded so loudly in her head that for a second or two she didn't actually realise that it had been echoed out loud—and by a totally different voice from her own.

'No, damn you! No way! You leave her alone!'

The next moment a large, powerful form came up behind her. Strong hands clamped over Miguel's arms, long fingers biting in hard. Miguel was wrenched away from her, flung back against the wall, his furious roar blending with the instinctive scream of fright that had been torn from her throat.

'And why the hell should I do as you say?'

'Because she's mine!' the tall, dark and very angry man who had suddenly arrived on the scene flung at him. 'Because she's not your woman—she's mine!'

'What?'

Even as Mercedes managed to get the single word out, she was caught up in a strong pair of arms, gathered close to a broad, hard chest. And in the same minute she realised that her scream had clearly been heard inside the house. There was a sudden silence, followed by a flurry of movement. The sound of many feet on the steps, on the flagstones. Hurrying feet. All heading in their direction.

'Oh, no.'

Mercedes' heart sank. Her one hope of keeping this quiet and covered up had been shattered in an instant.

'Oh, yes.'

The sound of an unpleasantly familiar voice made her feel even worse, a groan of despair escaping her as she saw just who had intervened so dramatically.

'You!'

Jake Taverner turned one swift glare on her, his light coloured eyes gleaming eerily in the moonlight.

'Me,' he returned succinctly. 'Who else?'

'Mercedes?' Miguel was furious. 'Who—?'

But his interjection was ignored as Mercedes and Jake glared at each other in fury.

'Just what do you think you were doing?'

'I think that's my question!' Jake shot back. 'What the hell do you think *you* were doing?'

'I was…Whatever I was doing, it was nothing at all to do with you!'

'Oh, no?'

'No. Nothing!'

She actually stamped her foot hard on the ground, needing some active way to express the anger that was boiling up inside her. Anger mixed with a terrible sense of humiliation and an added dash of despair at the realisation that, once again, she'd got herself into a real mess where Jake Taverner was concerned.

'How dare you interfere—?'

'What?' Jake parried scornfully. 'You wanted me to leave you here? With *him*?'

The toss of his head in the direction of the discomfited Miguel was a gesture of pure contempt.

'*That* was what you said I didn't measure up to?'

'I told you…'

The words shrivelled on her lips as she suddenly realised just what he had said as he had launched himself at the pair of them.

'You—I—what—how *dare* you?'

The memory of the impossible words drove all hope of speaking coherently away from her.

*Because she's not your woman—she's mine!*

'How dare I what?' he challenged brutally.

'Call me yours—your woman! I'm not—how dare you?' she could only repeat inanely.

'Oh, I dare,' Jake tossed back at her. 'When there's unfinished business between us—'

'There's nothing between us! Nothing!'

And to prove it she was getting out of here. The first of the people alerted by her scream were already reaching them, and, as if fate were determined to make matters as dreadful as possible for her, she could see that heading the rush were her two brothers Joaquin and Alex, with—heaven help her!— her father close behind.

'There's nothing between us,' she said again, with dark emphasis, forcing the words from between clenched teeth. 'And never will be.'

She was turning as she spoke, desperate to get away. But Jake wasn't going to let her go. Even as she swung round,

he was reaching for her, grabbing her by the arms again and
yanking her back close to him. She was crushed up against
his chest, glaring up into the cold blue eyes, feeling the heat
of his body, the way that his broad chest rose and fell so
rapidly with the disordered breathing that was the result of a
ferocious temper only barely reined in.

'You are going nowhere, sweetheart!' he growled roughly.
'You and I have things to talk about.'

'No, we don't! I have nothing to say to you and you can't
tell me anything I want to hear!'

At the end of her tether, she was beyond thinking what
she was doing. All she wanted was to get out of here and
away. Away before her brothers reached them and started
asking awkward questions. Before her father...

Wildly she launched a flailing kick at his nearer leg, only
succeeding in floundering awkwardly and clumsily. And Jake
had her imprisoned. His grip was too hard, too bruising to
break easily, and he was clearly not about to loosen it in a
hurry.

'Be reasonable, Mercedes.'

Jake's calm demeanour was totally infuriating, driving
Mercedes over the edge.

Reasonable! He thought this was *reasonable*, did he?

'You dare talk to me about being reasonable! *You!* When
you're trying to claim that I'm yours—you're as bad as
Miguel!'

'No!' It was furiously indignant.

'Yes!'

She had to make it loud, had to make it forceful because
even as she spoke she knew that her stupid, treacherous body
was responding to the strength and closeness of his. The arms
that held her so easily were the arms that had held her on
that night in London; held her in such a very different way.

'You're every bit as bad.'

In desperation she lifted her hands, clenching them into

tight, tight fists, then brought them thudding down on the stubborn, unyielding, hard, straight shoulders above her.

'Because I'm not yours—not in any way! I—I don't even want you!' she yelled, fists thumping against the fine cloth of his morning coat to punctuate each word. 'I—do—not—want—you!'

'That's not what you were saying in my bed the other night!' Jake shot back furiously. 'Then it was—"Jake, *amante*, Jake, *querido*—Jake, I want you now!"'

To Mercedes' horror the words fell into one of those stunned, shocking silences that almost made them echo around the moonlit courtyard. She saw Miguel's head come up, saw the furious glare he directed at her face, the total rejection stamped onto his dark features. He would never forgive her for this, she knew.

'Jake, you pig!'

In desperation she struggled in his arms again, hating the thought of being seen with him like this.

'Let me go! I—oh!'

She broke off on a cry of shock as there was a shout, a blur of movement. Someone caught hold of her from behind. Two masculine figures appeared, one either side of Jake, taking hold of his arms and wrenching him away.

There was an ugly little struggle. In the middle of it, Mercedes was whirled around, hauled up against another strong chest.

'It's all right, Mercedes,' a deep voice said. 'You're safe now.'

A voice she recognised. Her father's voice.

But there was something wrong. Something in his tone that made her nerves twist, her senses quail.

Blinking hard in shock, she stared up into her father's face, saw it change to hard, cold anger. Not quite knowing what was going on, she nerved herself to turn and follow the direction of that furious glare.

And saw Jake held in the tight grip of her two brothers. Their faces were hard and set in cold lines of anger and she had the dreadful feeling that they were determined to do him real damage if she didn't act fast.

She couldn't let that happen. Hate him as she did, she couldn't let her brothers take their anger out on Jake when he hadn't really done anything to deserve it—at least not tonight.

'No—you don't understand! Alex—Joaquin…'

'It's all right, little sister,' Joaquin grated. 'We've got him. He won't hurt you now.'

'But…'

She didn't know what to say, how to explain. But then the sight of Miguel—the real culprit in tonight's ugly farce— creeping away under cover of darkness made up her mind for her.

'No—you don't understand—he—Jake—it was all just a mistake.'

'No mistake.'

This time it was Jake who cut in. His arms might be held down at his sides, he might be her brothers' prisoner, but his proud dark head was still arrogantly high, the steely blue of his eyes blazing into her shocked brown ones.

'Jake…' Mercedes tried, glaring at him as fiercely as she dared, wanting to warn him, wanting him to shut up; wishing he would just leave this for her sake—and his own.

He didn't know her brothers and her father. As the baby of the family, and the only daughter as well, she had been cosseted and treasured from the moment she had been born. The tragically early death of her mother had only emphasised that situation, making Joaquin and her father turn to her to try and fill the empty space her mother had left behind. She had been spoiled rotten and she knew it, and her brothers' devotion to their 'little sister' was often blinded by love rather than following the clear light of realism.

But Jake clearly wasn't prepared to listen.

'No mistake,' he repeated with cold clarity.

She could glare at him all she wanted; he'd had enough of the little tease trying to pretend that she didn't know him—that they'd never met. Oh, she could pout and stamp her neat little foot, and turn those furious 'How dare you even breathe the same air as me?' blazing dark eyes on him in an attempt to squash him, but she'd soon find that he was completely uncrushable.

Better women than her had tried in the past. Tried and failed miserably.

And he wasn't going to let Mercedes Alcolar get away with any such thing. Particularly not after the way she had treated him.

'No mistake at all—unless of course you mean that you've got the wrong man.'

Turning to face the older brother—Joaquin, wasn't it?—he matched the tall Spaniard glare for glare, cool blue eyes clashing with furious dark.

'I wasn't the one who was manhandling your "little sister".'

'So what was that I saw when I got here?' Joaquin demanded, cold fury sounding in his tone as his grip tightened on Jake's arm. 'It looked to me like—'

'When you got here, Mercedes was the one attacking me,' Jake put in with cold reason. 'As I recall, she was the one who was thumping me with her fists—hard,' he added, with a wry twist of his lips at the memory.

'With good reason!' Mercedes protested, and Jake felt the other brother—Alex—move closer pointedly. 'You were—you were...'

'I was what?' Jake questioned icily when she hesitated, blushing in consternation. 'Just what was I doing that was so wrong?'

Deep brown eyes, turned molten bronze with anger, glared

straight at Jake as Mercedes struggled with the problem of just what it was safe for her to say.

'I came between you and Hernandez. Are you saying—?'

'If my daughter was with Miguel Hernandez,' Juan Alcolar put in, the cold arrogance of his voice clearly intended as a deliberate put-down, 'then why should it be anything to you?'

That tone was like the flick of a whip to Jake. It seemed to epitomise everything he had ever been told about Juan Alcolar. He could well believe what his mother had said about the way this man had treated her sister, not once, but twice.

'Mercedes and that young man have—an understanding.'

'Not any more.'

It was Miguel who spoke. He had been watching everything silently from his place by the wall, but now he moved forward, his malicious intent evident in the cold glitter in his eyes, the curl of his lip.

'If you ever hoped that I would marry your daughter, Alcolar,' he declared coldly, directing his words straight into Mercedes' father's watchful face, 'then you can forget the whole idea! The engagement is off. I don't want soiled goods, and tonight I have just discovered that your daughter—my future bride—has been unfaithful to me! That while she was in London she was also in this man's bed!'

# CHAPTER EIGHT

SHE was living in a nightmare.

It couldn't be true—it just couldn't! She had to be asleep—though heaven knew how or when. She had to have fallen asleep somewhere, somehow and tumbled straight into this horrible, appalling dream. And now she couldn't get out of it.

The worst part of it was the sudden total, stony silence that had descended following Miguel's outburst. A silence that made her look round reluctantly and realise just how many people had actually come out in response to her scream. People who were now gathered in a semicircle, staring at her, watching and waiting for her response.

Oh, please let this be a dream. And please let her wake up *soon*!

She tried pinching herself hard on the hand but that did nothing but hurt.

She wished that the ground would open up and swallow her whole. Anything that would get her out of here; take her away from this dreadful embarrassment, this terrible shame and make it all go away.

If only she *could* wake up and find it had never happened.

But that was never going to be. And, she realised on a shudder of horror, she wasn't going to be able to deny Miguel's accusation either. She couldn't if she wanted to. For one thing she was no good at lying. If she even tried then one of her family—her father or one of her brothers—would see straight through her pretence and guess at the truth.

The reality was that even if she thought she could give it a try, she'd lost her chance already. She'd hesitated too long,

condemned herself by her silence. If she had been able to
deny it, then her rejection would have come straight out,
instantly responding to Miguel's accusation—denying it
without even having to think.

Her silence might as well have been an admission. She
could see that on the faces of everyone around them; in the
indrawn breaths, the sudden whispers.

It was there in the way that her brothers' grasp on Jake's
arms had eased, too. They hadn't actually released him, but
their grip wasn't quite so punishing, the tightness in their
muscles lessening.

'Mercedes…'

It was her father who asked, everyone else keeping tact-
fully silent.

What could she say? What was there to say? If she denied
it further, what other appalling thing might Miguel go on to
say? And… The taste of humiliation was bitter in her mouth
as she remembered that Jake had brought 'evidence' along
with him. The hand on the arm that Alex held was dangerously close to the pocket from where, if he chose, she knew
that a sliver of pale blue silk could be produced to even more
damning effect.

'Well, yes,' Mercedes admitted reluctantly. 'But not in the
way you think!'

'What other way is there?'

She had never seen her father look at her in this way.
Never before felt the sting of his disapproval, the discomfort
of seeing his dark eyes cold and withdrawn.

But what had she expected? He was Juan Alcolar, after
all. A man to whom his Catalan heritage and his family name
meant everything. The reputation of that family name was
always uppermost in his thoughts. And Miguel's accusation
had just put that family name into a very bad light in front
of the large crowd of guests at this elegant society wedding.

He might not be as bad as old Alfredo Medrano, whose

daughter her brother Ramón had just married, but he was still very much of the old school. He might have accepted Joaquin's former mistress—now wife—into the family, but what Juan Alcolar's son got up to in private on his estate was one thing. The reputation of his only daughter being called into question by the man she had been expected to marry, in a very public place, was a very different matter.

Particularly when a large part of the assembled audience were members of the same society who had ostracised Ramón's new wife because of a youthful transgression.

'I—' she began protestingly, but it was clear that her father was not prepared to discuss the matter any further.

'We will talk about this later—in private.'

'*Papá!*'

'Later.'

'But…'

Her father's glare swept round the staring crowd, then came back to her, cold-eyed. He was obviously fighting for control.

'Enough.'

His hand came up and slashed through the air as if cutting off the conversation sharply.

'I have said I do not want to talk about it here.'

It was his last word on the subject; Mercedes could have no doubt about that. Already he was turning, preparing to walk away, gathering the cloak of his dignity around him as he always did when something threatened his composure and his status.

'Would it help if I told you that we were engaged?'

The question came from the last possible source she had expected—from Jake himself.

It was out of the blue, so startling that it stilled everyone, even her father. He actually paused with one foot out, ready for the next step, and then slowly turned back.

'What did you say?'

Jake took his time.

For a start he turned his head, right and left, looking down
pointedly at the spots where Alex and Joaquin still held him.
He didn't have to say anything but they got the point, re-
leasing their grip on his arms and letting him go. They even
stepped back, which made Mercedes shiver faintly. Alex and
Joaquin wouldn't back down to anyone, so they must have
recognised something in this man that demanded their re-
spect.

'I said would it help matters if I told you that we—
Mercedes and I—are engaged?'

The blue eyes locked with Mercedes, challenging her to
contradict him. To deny his assertion. But she was still too
stunned, too bemused by everything that had happened to
even process the facts. Had he really claimed that they…?

'You asked her to marry you?' her father questioned, glaring even more ferociously, the bite of anger in his words.
'And she said yes?'

'That is what the word engaged usually means.'

Jake was clearly not at all prepared to back down or even
give a little. He met Juan eye to eye, his dark head held every
bit as high and proud as the older man's. Without even looking away, he brushed down the sleeves of his beautifully
tailored jacket where her brothers' grip had crushed it, re-
storing the lie of the fine material to its former smooth elegance.

'And are you still engaged?'

'Why don't you ask her?'

Once more the light coloured gaze flicked to Mercedes'
face, just briefly, and then away again. But she felt that she
understood—though she didn't know why. For some reason,
known only to himself, Jake was suddenly giving her the
chance to redeem herself in her father's eyes. It was up to
her whether she took it or not, his quick, flashing glance said.

'Mercedes?'

Her father had turned to her, a look of enquiry on his face.

'Are you engaged to this man?'

Twice Mercedes opened her mouth to answer him, and each time her voice failed her. She didn't dare to look in Jake's direction, fearing that the direct, unyielding look in the cool, clear eyes would drive every thought from her head, leaving her incapable of forming a word.

'We had a row, didn't we?' Jake prompted.

'Mmm.' It was all that she could manage.

'And you left and came back here—refusing to see me again.'

'Yes—that's right.'

That much at least she could say yes to, and mean it. That wasn't a lie.

'And I came after her to beg her to reconsider...'

But now Jake was just taking things way too far.

'You...'

Mercedes' head swung round in horror and she glared at him in furious reproof. He met the blaze of her eyes with unrepentant nonchalance.

'But when I found her in the garden with Miguel, I'm afraid I lost my temper.'

To Mercedes' horror, he was walking towards her—and no one was stopping him! On the contrary, her father simply watched and Alex—damn him!—Alex had a small, smug smile on his face that made her grit her teeth against the urge to demand just what he was grinning at.

'Perhaps we could go somewhere quieter to talk about this? I'm sure we've both made mistakes, Mercedes.'

He made it sound appallingly reasonable. *He* sounded so reasonable, Mercedes thought in panic.

Because, from the looks of things, he was winning everyone over. The mood of the crowd that had gathered at her foolish scream and who still lingered had changed perceptibly. Tense, concerned, disapproving expressions, expressions that had changed to critical censure at Miguel's accusation, had now eased into something nearer blatant curiosity.

*A lovers' tiff.*

She could almost hear them saying it; read their thoughts in their eyes. A squabble between an engaged couple. Something that would cause a buzz of gossip for days to come, but not the scandal they had thought it might be. And she would be risking making it look like so much more if she rejected Jake's apparent apology now. She didn't dare to draw attention to herself any more. After all, this was the set of society people who had made her brand new sister-in-law Estrella's life such a misery until she had gained respectability by marrying Ramón. They would do the same to her if they so much as got the sniff of something to use against her.

And if she denied it, then Jake had something else in his armoury.

Was it deliberate, the way that his hand was still resting lightly on that left-hand pocket of his jacket? The pocket that she knew still kept concealed her underwear, the sliver of silk that he was capable of producing—of displaying to the audience he now held in the palm of his hand, shaming and embarrassing her for ever in their eyes.

'Mistakes...'

The truth was that the engagement had already been accepted by everyone. She could tell it from their faces, the relaxation of tension all around them. And in spite of trying to gather all her courage, it was quite beyond her to risk stirring up trouble again. Not here, not now, not tonight.

She supposed she should be grateful to Jake for the way he had claimed she was engaged to him. She couldn't begin to imagine why he had done that. But an engagement could be broken, couldn't it? It wasn't for ever. She'd take the easy way out tonight and tomorrow would be another day.

She would deal with Jake Taverner tomorrow.

\*     \*     \*

Jake didn't know just why he had claimed to be engaged to
Mercedes. He'd acted in the same, instinctive way that he
had when he'd seen her obviously in trouble with Miguel
Hernandez; when he'd claimed her as his in front of the other
man. He only knew that it had had the effect he had hoped
for and got the crowd to lose interest in what was going on.
Already their audience was beginning to break up, drift back
towards the lighted ballroom where there was still plenty of
champagne to be drunk, and the band to dance to. What had
looked like a potential scandal to set their tongues wagging
had turned out to be nothing more than a lovers' tiff.

But it could all have been so very different. The anger on
the faces of Mercedes' brothers when they'd grabbed hold of
him had been real enough—and he could feel the bruises on
his arms as a result. And Papá Alcolar had been furious—
outraged at the way that his daughter had become embroiled
in the unseemly events at the centre of it all. He had looked
as if he was ready to disown her as a result.

Which was the Alcolars all over. If someone didn't fit with
what they thought was their due—if someone wasn't, in their
opinion, good enough for them—they dropped them fast and
without so much as a second thought.

And Mercedes had looked so lost, so stunned by her father's response that he had suddenly found himself taking
pity on her and coming out with the fantasy engagement
without thinking.

But that didn't mean he was letting her off the hook.

'Mistakes,' she hissed in response to his comment. 'We—
you—'

'Mercedes,' her father cut in, the coldness not yet fully
erased from his voice, the words still stiff with disapproval
and anger. 'Won't you introduce us to your—fiancé?'

She winced at the sound of that word, Jake noted. But
whether it was at the fact that she was trapped in a situation
that was none of her making or because she hated the thought

of being linked with him in this way, he had no way of knowing. Whatever she felt, it earned him another flashing glare of reproof as she struggled to answer her parent.

'This is Jake...Jake Taverner.'

She managed to make it sound like a description of something particularly disgusting, her mouth curling in distaste on his name, her tongue seeming to tangle up over it.

And she clearly wasn't at all happy when her father pounced on the name with relish.

'Taverner? Are you anything to do with Taverner Telecommunications?'

'He *is* Taverner Telecommunications,' Mercedes said grudgingly. 'That was how we met—at a media party.'

'And I was knocked for six by your daughter's beauty,' Jake put in, carefully steering the conversation away from the dangerous waters of his name and background.

It was a damn good thing that his mother had only married Ralph Taverner after her sister's death. As a result, Juan Alcolar would have no cause to link Marguerite Dario and her sister Elizabeth Jensen with the Taverner media empire.

'But unfortunately we fell out over something and nothing—'

'Something and no—!' Mercedes exploded. 'Why, you—!'

'Hush, sweetheart!'

Jake laid a hand over her mouth to silence her, managing to make it look like a lover's gesture while actually exerting enough force to squash the tirade of objection that she was clearly longing to fling in his face.

'I know that to you it was something...'

Her blazing eyes told him that the phoney loving tone, the hint of gentle reproach, had only infuriated her further, even if they had convinced her father. He would suffer for this later, that angry glare told him. She would get her revenge any way she could.

But until then, he had the upper hand and he was determined to use it.

She didn't dare contradict him now, he knew. If she had meant to expose his story as a lie then she should have done as soon as he'd told it. Now it was way too late and would require too many complicated explanations, none of which would meet with her family's approval, or, clearly, that of the society in which she lived.

'But can't we forget about it for tonight at least?'

Behind them, Joaquin Alcolar stirred, moving forward.

'I think it's time we all went in and carried on with the party,' he said firmly. 'This is supposed to be a wedding celebration, after all. We'll leave you and Mercedes alone, Taverner. It seems to me you have things to talk out.'

And he didn't envy Jake the experience, his expression and his tone said only too clearly. Clearly Mercedes thought so too as she diverted her angry gaze from Jake's face to her brother's and snatched in a breath as she struggled to free her mouth enough to protest.

'You go in,' Jake told the few lingering members of their audience hastily, knowing that if he lost his grip on her all hell would break loose. 'We'll be with you in a minute.'

The momentary distraction as he watched her father and brothers head back towards the *castillo* gave Mercedes a tiny advantage. Wrenching her mouth away from his covering hand, she turned to yell after her retreating family.

'Wait! Don't leave—'

She never managed to complete the sentence. Grabbing at her chin and forcing her face round to his again, Jake squashed the rest of the words back down her throat as he covered her mouth with his and kissed her into silence with a punishing force and passion that crushed her lips hard under his, making her grunt slightly in shock and protest.

With one eye on the progress of her family, he held her there for just as long as he wanted, restraining her struggles with an insulting lack of effort, and only when she stopped fighting him did he ease up on his grip.

And then he kissed her properly.

Kissed her as he had been wanting to do from the moment she had walked into the church in that smart blue suit. Kissed her as he remembered kissing her that first time, back in London, in the dining room of his house. Kissed her as his hungry body had been demanding ever since he had come out into the garden and seen her there, with Miguel's arms around her, his disgusting wandering hands tracing the delectable lines of her body.

'Mercedes…' He husked her name deep in his throat and her only response was a sigh, soft and low.

It was every bit as amazing as he remembered. She tasted wonderful; she smelt wonderful; she felt wonderful. Just the sensation of her mouth under his made his thoughts swim. And when she suddenly and unexpectedly stopped fighting him, her lips softening, opening, letting him in, he felt that burning need rise in him again, heating his blood and making him harder and hungrier than he had ever been before.

So hard, so hungry that his primitive, instinctive impulse was to pull her down with him, onto the hard, cold ground if necessary, and take her then and there, giving into the erotic urgings of his passion.

He even moved closer on the thought, gathering her to him in a lover's embrace, not a captor's. His arms around her tightened in a very different way, his heart jerked in his chest, and his breathing roughened, becoming rawly uneven as his tongue invaded the sweet softness of her mouth, tangling with hers in a hungry intimacy.

And the effect on Mercedes was disastrous. From being softly willing, pliant and responsive, she suddenly jolted back to reality in the space of a second. Her slender body stiffened, moved as far away from his as was possible within the confines of his arms, and she twisted her head frantically, struggling to free herself from his kiss.

And in the space of a heartbeat common sense reasserted itself, exerting a vital restraint.

Now was not the time. Here was not the place.

But there would be a time and a place at some point in the future, he promised himself.

And when that time came then she would be willing. Not fighting. Not struggling. Not pulling back, her body stiff and frozen as a board. She would be warm and she would be welcoming. As welcoming as she had been to him on that night in his apartment in London.

That he could wait for. He reckoned it would be well worth the wait.

But for now he had to win her family round, too. They had given him a restrained welcome at the news that he had asked Mercedes to marry him. More in his favour had been the news that he owned Taverner Telecommunications. But if they realised that he was not just Ramón's friend, but also his cousin, and a member of the Jensen family—the family that had vowed never to rest until they saw Juan Alcolar brought as low as he had brought Jake's mother's sister—then everything would change. Even those polite, meaningless social smiles would fade and he would find himself out in the cold again, with the heavy wooden doors of their society closed in his face.

A lukewarm welcome might be all that he was getting right now. But lukewarm was better than cold—it was most definitely better than nothing.

And so as he watched Mercedes' father and her two brothers step back into the light and music of the ballroom he clamped down hard on the heated demands of his hungry body, and forced himself to raise his head, abandoning Mercedes' mouth and looking down into her deep, dark eyes, shadowed in the moonlight.

'I think we'd better follow them. If I read your father right, then he'll only allow us so much leeway—engaged couple or not.'

'We're not engaged, and you know it! You lied.'

'No lie, *señorita*,' he reproved with infuriating mock gentleness. 'I never said anything was so—just asked if it would make things better if we were engaged. Your father took the rest of it and ran with it.'

'As you knew damn well he would!'

Mercedes knew that deep down she was snarling at herself and not at him—or, at least, only half Jake and very definitely the other half at herself.

She couldn't believe what she had just done. That after all that had happened, after the way he had treated her, the way he had manipulated the situation here and with her father, she had been so weak as to react as she had when he had kissed her.

'I don't want to be engaged to you! I don't want anything to do with you!'

'So you'd rather I had told your father and brothers—and assorted friends, neighbours and hangers-on—that you jumped into my bed for a one-night stand? No,' he answered his own question as he saw her face change. 'Of course you wouldn't. So we're engaged. It suits me and it suits you.'

'But that's just the point I don't get! Why should it suit you?'

Jake's mouth twisted and he rubbed his arms where Alex and Joaquin had held him prisoner.

'If you had had your two hulking brutes of brothers holding you down and glaring at you with murder in their eyes at the thought you had besmirched their precious little sister's honour, believe me, you'd have said anything to make them back off.'

It was only when the tiny, barely formed flame of hope in her heart sadly guttered and died that Mercedes even realised it had been there. But the empty hole it left told her just what she had been hoping for—and just how foolish she had been even to think of it.

Had she really been letting herself dream that Jake might have had some vaguely charitable reason for claiming their engagement? That he had done it to protect her, defend her from the cold disapproval, the social ostracism that, like Estrella, she might have received otherwise?

She had to have been all sorts of a fool if she had! He had acted only out of pure self-interest—with the aim of defending himself from the anger of her father and brothers. She hadn't even figured in his reasoning at all. And if she had been weak enough even to let the idea into her mind—and, even worse, into her heart—that only made matters so much worse.

'And did you kiss me to put my brothers off, too?'

That brought a darkly satanic grin onto Jake's strong-boned face. A grin that curled his mouth but did nothing at all to light up his eyes.

'No, that was to stop you shouting out and ruining everything. How do you think it would have looked if I'd just persuaded them we were engaged—madly in love—and yet you were afraid to be left alone with me?'

And he had watched her family walk away, waiting calculatedly until they had been out of sight and out of earshot, before he had stopped kissing her.

The knowledge slashed at the emptiness that was a cruel wound in her heart, opening it wider, deeper, more painful than before.

She had done it again! She had let him lead her on, as he had done on that night in London. He had only to touch her, kiss her and she had melted like wax in the heat.

One kiss and her heart had been racing, her blood pulsing. She had felt as if she had been standing in the fierce heat of midday instead of the cooler, paler light of the moon. She had put so much of herself into that kiss, unable to hold back, but all it had been to him was a calculated way of keeping her quiet, stopping her from spoiling his plans.

But what were his plans? What was he going to get out of this pretend engagement?

'Why should I let you get away with this?' she demanded. 'What's to stop me going straight in there to tell everyone the truth?'

Jake folded his arms, leaned back against a tree and studied her indignant face, her anger-bright eyes. He actually seemed to be considering, but there was an expression on his stunning features that warned her he already had his answer to hand and the delay was all for show.

'Your reputation,' he pronounced at last. 'Your good name—at home and in the neighbourhood. Your father's approval.'

He'd hit home with that one, Mercedes acknowledged privately, wincing at the barbed comment. He must have seen her face, noted her reaction earlier and now he was using that knowledge to his own advantage.

'And how about—?'

'All right, all right! You've made your point! I'm stuck with you.'

'We're stuck with each other.'

That carefully reasonable tone really grated. Mercedes felt as if the words had stripped away a fine but much-needed layer of skin, leaving the delicate nerves underneath raw and open.

'We can't do this! I can't! It's all a pretence—none of it's real.'

'But they don't know that,' Jake pointed out with a nod of his head back towards the *castillo*. 'And as long as we both play our parts carefully, there's no reason why anyone should find out.'

Mercedes stared at him in bewilderment and doubt. Just

what was going on inside that handsome head? What thoughts were buzzing in the cool, incisive mind that had reacted so swiftly and so effectively earlier to diffuse a situation that had become dangerously explosive?

'And—and how long will we have to "play our parts" for?'

Once again Jake appeared to consider, though this time she was more than ever convinced that he knew exactly what he was going to say.

'As long as it takes.'

'To do what?'

The sexy mouth twitched, as if he'd been about to break into a grin but then had ruthlessly suppressed the impulse.

'Until I get what I want.'

'Until…'

Should she ask? Did she even want to? Mercedes doubted that she really wanted to know, but she couldn't stop herself.

'And just what is it that you want out of this?'

This time the grin couldn't be held back but broke, wide and devilish, in a flash of white teeth in the moonlight.

'Oh, Mercedes, haven't you worked it out yet? I would have thought that it was obvious.'

'Not to me, it isn't,' Mercedes snapped, her voice tart with tension. 'You'll have to spell it out.'

So he did.

'What I want out of this, Mercedes, my darling, is you. I want you in my bed, as my mistress. Always have done from the first moment I saw you—and nothing has changed. I want you, and I intend to get you, one way or another.'

# CHAPTER NINE

MERCEDES yawned, stretched and rubbed her hands viciously over her eyes in an attempt to wake herself up, make herself feel a bit more human.

A vain attempt. She couldn't have felt less awake, less human if she'd tried. Five nights without much sleep could do that to you.

Five nights spent tossing and turning, unable to get comfortable, unable to doze off.

Five nights spent lying on her back—when she wasn't tossing and turning—staring at the white-painted ceiling trying to think of a way out.

Trying *not* to think of Jake.

Just the thought of Jake was guaranteed to drive all hope of sleep away from her mind, no matter how exhausted she had made her body during the day.

And she had *tried*.

She had tried.

From the moment she had had to go back into the ballroom on the evening of Ramón's wedding, she had been trying, one way or another, to get Jake Taverner out of her mind— and failing miserably.

It had been impossible to do anything that night, because Jake's insistence on them playing the part of a newly engaged couple had forced her into a closeness to him that she detested. It had meant that she'd had to stay by his side, and hadn't been able to get away at all.

So she had danced with him, talked with him, forcing a smile and pretence of interest on her face until she'd felt as if her tight muscles would crack under the strain. She had drunk champagne—too much champagne—with him and could only be grateful that she had done so when, to her horror, her father had decided to make an announcement.

'You all know that tonight is in fact the celebration of the marriage of one of my sons—Ramón—to his beautiful bride Estrella,' Juan said, standing on the dais in the centre of the huge ballroom where the band had been performing. 'But some of you may be unaware that, for my family, it also marks another cause for celebration...'

'Oh, no!' Mercedes muttered under her breath. 'Please, no! Oh, *Papá*, don't!'

But of course her father didn't hear her. And if he had, she had no doubt that he wouldn't have heeded her. He was determined on making this announcement and nothing was going to stand in his way.

'I can now make public that, to my intense joy, my beloved only daughter, Mercedes, has announced her engagement—to Jake Taverner of Taverner Telecommunications.'

'Smile!' a voice hissed behind her, making her aware that Jake, thankfully absent from her side for a few much-needed moments, had come back to play the devoted fiancé once again.

'I don't feel like smiling,' Mercedes muttered out of the corner of her mouth, knowing that her words would be concealed from anyone but him by the round of applause that broke out in response to her father's announcement.

'Neither do I, but it's expected of us—so *smile*!'

An arm snaked round her waist, pulling her close up against the hard warmth of his body, and out of the corner of her eye she saw Jake lift his champagne glass in response to the toasts and calls of congratulations directed their way.

Weakly she tried to do the same, forcing her unwilling mouth to curve upwards, her cheeks to crease into something that she prayed looked remotely like the smile that Jake had demanded.

Jake Taverner—*of Taverner Telecommunications*. Of course her father had had to get that point in. He would consider it such a coup, and he would want everyone there to know it. Not only had Ramón's marriage brought Estrella's father's television company as part of the bride's dowry, but now she too was connecting the Alcolar media empire with the huge British enterprise.

Or at least that was how he believed the future was going to be. Deep inside, Mercedes shivered faintly at the thought of just what would happen when he found out the truth.

The shiver deepened, turned into an actual shudder as she felt Jake move, sensed the touch of his warm breath on the delicate skin on the back of her neck, lifting all the fine hairs in immediate response. A moment later the soft pressure of his mouth against the already sensitised flesh made her knees threaten to buckle, only the strength of Jake's arm, still tightly round her waist, holding her upright as he kissed his way along the line of her upper spine.

'That was a neat bit of damage limitation,' he murmured against her skin, making her throat dry and her head swim disturbingly. 'Just in case there was any hangover from the fuss outside, your *papá* made sure that everyone knows the real story.'

'But it isn't the *real* story!' Mercedes hissed, her mind seeming to split in two, the desire to break away from his controlling grip warring with the need to sink back weakly and simply let him kiss her. 'And you damn well know it!'

'It is for now,' Jake informed her, blithely ignoring the furious protest in her voice. 'So can I suggest that you go along with it before anyone notices that you look more like someone with a violent case of indigestion than the ecstatic, overjoyed bride-to-be you're supposed to be, and starts to wonder just what's wrong?'

'I'd be only too happy to tell them!'

'Liar,' Jake reproved with deadly gentleness. 'Right now

you'd rather die than admit to such a public humiliation. So why don't you make some effort to at least make this look realistic? And then, if you're really good, I'll let you punish me later—in private.'

The rich, dark sensuality in his tone left Mercedes in no doubt as to just what he imagined that 'punishment' would consist of and the image was so potently erotic that it went straight to what was left of her brain like a draught of the most potent spirit, intoxicating her in seconds.

In an effort to control her thoughts, she dug sharp white teeth down into the rosy swell of her bottom lip, forcing back the betraying moan of response that threatened to escape her.

How could he know her so well? She had only spent three short days—and then not the full twenty-four hours in any of them—in this man's company and yet already he could read her like a book. He almost seemed to be able to interpret her thoughts, predict what she was about to say, how she was feeling. And he used that knowledge mercilessly, manipulating the situation—and her—exactly the way he wanted it.

So did he know that with his arm still around her like this, the feel of his mouth still lingering on the tender skin at the back of her neck, she was highly, scorchingly aroused, and struggling desperately to conceal it? He must do. How could he not know it?

Perhaps he knew it and deep down inside that was what he wanted too?

He must know how she longed to let her head drop back against his shoulder. How she wished those tormenting lips would move, take her own mouth in one of those searingly passionate kisses that wrenched her soul out of her body and set her heart thundering like the most violent storm. He could surely sense how she wished the whole ballroom, and all the people in it, would just disappear, evaporate, leaving nothing in the world but her and this man. This man who could turn her into someone else entirely; someone she didn't know or recognise. In his arms the rational, controlled Mercedes disappeared and in her place was a wild, wanton, passionate woman whose desires could only barely be held in check.

So now, in her bed, Mercedes stirred, restless, unsettled, even by just the memory of the way she had felt then. The covers were way too hot, too heavy, and she flung them aside with a muttered curse, not caring that they went right over the other side of the bed and fell in a crumpled heap on the floor.

She had wanted more than just Jake's arms around her. And she had been so sure that that was what he'd wanted too. So much so that in another moment she would have given in to her needs, turning until she was face to face with him, pressing herself up against him, lifting her mouth to his…

But she hadn't. Somehow she had fought with herself hard enough to hold herself still, though every nerve in her body had screamed an angry protest at the torment she'd been inflicting on it by denying herself in that way. She hadn't given in to the sensual temptation that had tortured her, and now she could only thank God that she had managed to hold out against it. Because Jake's next comments had made it only too plain to her just what a fool she would have been to show him anything of the way she'd been feeling.

Because *his* mind had been on totally practical matters and on the need to maintain the fiction they had created in order to convince her family and friends. There had been nothing erotic or passionate in his thoughts at all.

'Perhaps you ought to know where I'm staying? It would look a little strange if my supposed fiancée had no idea where to find me after tonight was over—sort of Cinderella in reverse.'

'Of course,' she sighed, knowing he was right but wishing he weren't. 'Where will you be? What hotel?'

'No hotel. I'm staying in town. Ramón let me have his apartment while he's away.'

'Ramón? Oh—of course—you're here as his guest. So how do you come to know him? You never mentioned it before.'

'We're in the same business,' Jake hedged. If she realised how well he knew Ramón she might start putting two and two together and she could come up with a four that he just didn't want her to even consider.

'And he's letting you stay in his apartment—for how long?'

'I'm looking after it while he's away on honeymoon.'

'But he and Estrella will be gone for a month!'

'Then I'll be living in his flat for that month.'

He couldn't. Oh, please let it not be true! Let him be joking—making it up!

Too restless to stay still any longer, Mercedes got out of bed and walked to the window, pushing her hand through the long fall of her black silky hair.

She had thought that he would just stay a day or so—three at the very most. That she would only have to endure a few hours of each day playing his fiancée and then he would leave and go back to England and she would be free.

And after that?

Well, she'd decided, they could play it out a little longer, take it slowly, let the memory of the night in the *castillo* gardens fade in people's memories until it grew dim, and they started to forget, or some other potential scandal caught their attention, filled their minds. Then she could gradually drop hints that things were not going well; that she and Jake were arguing, having problems. She might even risk a trip to England, ostensibly to talk things over, try and put them right. But of course she would 'fail'.

She didn't even have to see Jake at any point. She just needed to say that she had.

And then she could come home with some story of how it had all gone terribly wrong—a dreadful row—they had broken up—no, it couldn't be mended, no hope of that at all. She might have to look a little wan and sad, but not for long.

And then it would all be over and she would be free.

Now that idea seemed like a hopeless, foolish dream. Instead she was going to be forced to play Jake's fiancée for the remainder of the four weeks while he lived in her brother's apartment only ten minutes' drive away from her own home.

She'd already spent five days playing a part that made her feel ill just to think of it. If the night of the wedding had been bad, then the days that had followed had been a sort of hell on earth. Jake had appeared at her home every single day, playing the devoted, attentive fiancé, and she had had to follow his lead in everything.

And the worst part was the way that her family seemed to have taken to him. Joaquin and Alex might have been friends with Jake for years, they got on so well. And even her father, while always aloof and remote with strangers, had seemed unusually affable.

Which made the part she was playing—the lie she was acting out—even worse.

She *couldn't* do it! She wouldn't!

But did she have any choice in the matter? Ever since she had stayed silent when Jake had claimed to be her fiancé, she had to all intents and purposes thrown in her lot with him. She would have to go along with this, whether she wanted to or not. The prospect of the next few weeks stretched ahead of her like some appalling prison sentence and she didn't know how she was going to endure it.

She *wasn't* going to endure it!

Filled with a new resolve, she swung away from the window and headed towards her wardrobe, pulling out clothes at random.

This couldn't go on any longer. She wouldn't let it! She was going to see Jake and tell him that she wasn't playing his game any more. She would demand that he stopped. That together they could find some way out of this.

Jake stood by the window in the living room of Ramón's apartment, coffee mug forgotten in his hand as he stared out at the city gradually coming to life in the cool light of dawn. Another few hours and the heat would build again, the sun blazing down on crowded, noisy streets. But for now, it was calm and quiet and he had time to think.

Of Mercedes.

There was only one topic that ever entered his head these days. Only one person he couldn't get out of his thoughts. Only one person he could never come any closer to understanding, no matter how many times he tried.

In fact, it seemed that the more he attempted to pin her down, the more she slipped away from his grasp and refused to be defined. It was like trying to dissect a rainbow—she just slipped through his fingers and disappeared. And all he was left with was a string of fleeting images, indefinable, and intangible, maddeningly frustrating.

He'd thought, when he'd set up the whole fiancée idea, that it would give him a chance to get to know her—to find the real Mercedes under the avalanche of contradictory images that had assailed him since the moment he had first met her. But instead she remained more elusive than ever.

She was like a superbly cut diamond—bright, brilliant, beautiful—but with so many facets to her character that each of them dazzled his eyes, blinding him to so many other, different aspects of her personality.

But he was still no nearer to knowing her.

The sound of a car down in the street, coming closer, drew his attention for a moment.

So he wasn't the only one awake in Barcelona at this early

hour. Briefly he wondered just what had brought the other person out of their bed before the sun had fully risen. Good news or bad? Were they heading out somewhere, starting their day early, or returning home after a night on the tiles?

His mouth twisted wryly as he remembered the many nights that he had arrived home at the same time as the milk delivery. Youth was to be enjoyed, he had always felt. Life was to be lived—and he had done plenty of living.

There had always been plenty of women too. Women who had wanted the same sort of enjoyment as he had, and who had never asked for commitment. He had never looked for for ever—or even for a guaranteed tomorrow. If things hadn't worked then they had said goodbye and gone their separate ways. It had all been very civilised.

Usually.

So why didn't he just turn and walk away from Mercedes?

He couldn't; that was the simple, the honest answer. He couldn't walk away, and even if he did he would never be able to get her out of his mind. He wanted her more than he had ever wanted any woman in his life and her very elusiveness only made that hunger worse, stoking the appetite with frustration and lack of fulfilment.

'Damnation!'

Jake brought his fist down onto the window-sill in a gesture of exasperation.

He had never given up on anything in his life. The firm that the Alcolar Corporation had beaten him to with their takeover bid was the only thing he hadn't managed to acquire when he'd wanted it. He wasn't going to let another Alcolar defeat him ever again.

Perhaps if Mercedes had stayed that night in London, if he had slept with her, known her intimately, then maybe he would have solved the puzzle of the effect she had on him, appeased the gnawing hunger she awoke in him. Then he could have gone on with his life and forgotten about her.

But, because she had disappeared like that, she had got under his skin in a way that he didn't think he could ever be free of until he had her in his bed.

And when he had her there? What then? Well, he'd wait and see if the fulfilment was as he imagined it would be. And then he'd answer that question.

But he had little doubt that she would be all that he had dreamed in the long, restless, hunger-filled nights that he had endured since she had run out on him that time. He had got so near and yet so far—he'd tasted enough of the delights of her body to know he could never rest until he'd known them all. Even in his dreams she wasn't truly his. He dreamed of taking her to his bed, of easing the clothes from her body, pressing his mouth to her skin, taking the warm, soft weight of her breasts in his eager hands...

'Hellfire,' he muttered furiously, shifting uncomfortably as the fit of the jeans that were all he wore became tight and uncomfortable as the erection even just his thoughts had produced strained against it.

He was always like this, these days. Always thinking of her—of Mercedes. Always hungry, always, always aroused, until he felt he could almost put back his head and howl like a wolf, baying at the moon in a wild, primitive expression of his need.

'Hell and damnation—this has got to end!'

It was either that or go completely, totally out of his mind.

The sound of the car had stopped. Obviously the other early riser had reached their destination, and it was somewhere close by.

Scowling down at the now cold and unappealing coffee in his mug, he was heading for the kitchen to replace it when the sound of the doorbell startled him into stillness.

'Who the hell?'

A quick glance at the clock confirmed that it was every bit as early as he had thought it was. He hadn't been standing lost in thought for so long that time had slid away far more quickly than he had anticipated.

'What…?'

The way he wrenched open the door reflected the niggling anxiety that was bubbling up inside him. He didn't know if this unexpected caller had come for him, or for Ramón as the owner of the apartment in which he was a temporary resident. He only knew that a visitor at this hour meant news of some sort, usually bad.

'You!'

The word exploded from him as he saw the tall, slender, dark-haired figure standing in the doorway. Mercedes Alcolar—but a Mercedes such as he had never seen before.

Like him, she had clearly just pulled on the nearest clothes to hand and the baggy tee shirt and elderly jeans were so unlike the elegant designer fashions he was used to seeing her in that for a second or two he blinked in something close to disbelief. Her hair tumbled around her face, looking as if she had only managed to pull a brush through it before she had left the house.

But it was her face that was so very different that he barely recognised her. She wore no make-up—none at all—and the golden complexion had a softness and a delicacy that no cosmetics could ever paint on it. The dark eyes still seemed smudged from sleep—or, rather, sleeplessness, faint shadows marking the skin beneath them—and the long, thick black lashes needed no artifice to enhance their lush and sensuous appeal. She looked ten years younger—almost childlike—impossibly innocent.

'What the hell are you doing here?'

He didn't care how aggressive, how hostile it sounded. He had been caught totally off balance and the polite social niceties were quite beyond him.

'We have to talk.'

*No, we don't…*

The thought was in his head before he had time to impose any degree of control. His eyes were devouring the sight of her, his other senses instantly on overdrive in response to her appearance so soon after the battle he had had to suppress his wild, erotic imaginings only moments earlier.

No, we don't have to talk. What we have to do is touch and caress, and feel. What you have to do is to come into my arms and let me kiss you until we're both out of our minds with need, until there isn't a thought that goes through our heads but you and me and...

Hell, *no*!

No!

He mustn't let his thoughts go that way.

Unless by some amazing miracle she had turned up here like this to say that she felt the same—that she'd tried but she couldn't go on any longer without him...

'Jake, did you hear what I said? We—'

'Yeah, yeah—we have to talk.'

It was a struggle, but somehow he managed to gather his scrambled, wandering thoughts and try to put them into some order—some *respectable* sort of order.

Of course she hadn't come here to say she felt the same. She had made it plain that she detested him, that she saw him as less than the dirt beneath her dainty little feet.

So why *was* she here?

'Talk about what?'

Mercedes' dark eyes swung to one side and then another, glancing along the landing outside the apartment, and when she looked back at him flames of furious reproach burned in their depths.

'You don't think I want to talk about it here—in public— do you?'

'Well, if you want to make things private...be my guest.'

Jake held the door open as wide as possible and stood well back so that she would not have to come close to him as she moved into the room. Just the thought of connecting the words *in private* with being alone with Mercedes set up a heady pounding of his blood that was hard enough to control. If she so much as touched him, then he wouldn't be answerable for the consequences.

'So,' he continued, shutting the door firmly again and leaning back against it, arms folded across his chest, his eyes fixed on her face, 'what exactly did you want to talk to me about?'

'I—I...' She stumbled over her words and bit down hard on her lower lip in obvious consternation.

'You?' Jake prompted harshly when it looked as if she would give up completely, unable to say anything more. 'You said you wanted to talk—so talk.'

She looked as if she would rather face a firing squad than speak, but eventually she swallowed hard and forced the answer out.

'I wanted to try and see if we could come to some sort of arrangement.'

'Oh, really? And just what sort of an arrangement did you have in mind?'

# CHAPTER TEN

*I WANTED to try and see if we could come to some sort of arrangement.*

Oh, dear heaven, why had she ever said that?

It wasn't what she'd meant to say. In fact it was almost the last thing Mercedes had ever *thought* of saying! But somehow, foolishly, without knowing why, she had blurted it out.

She didn't want to come to any sort of *arrangement*. Not with Jake—not under any circumstances! She had come here this morning to tell him that this whole stupid pretence was over. She was not going along with it any more. It had to stop right here and now—and for good.

She had come here to deliver an ultimatum: stop this travesty of an engagement—or else!

Her resolve had been strong and set. That resolve had driven her out of the house and into her car, keeping her determinedly on the road, heading here—straight here, no diversions or delays. She had even repeated her speech over and over to herself as she had come up in the lift.

But somehow, in the moment that the door had opened and she had seen Jake standing there, all her determination had evaporated—and so had those carefully rehearsed and repeated words.

'I—er...'

Just how was she supposed to think straight when the man was standing there half naked? The worn and faded jeans were clearly the only thing he had on and above them the broad expanse of his chest, dusted with curling dark hair, was a dangerously disturbing distraction.

She tried to look him in the face, but failed. Her eyes would keep moving to the straight, hard line of his shoulders, the power of his biceps, the play of muscle under the sleek skin as he folded and unfolded his arms. Her mouth was dry and she slicked a nervous tongue over parched, open lips.

'What sort of an arrangement?'

'One that—don't you think you'd better put some clothes on?'

Jake dropped one swift, frowning glance down at his exposed chest and then back up again, meeting her darkened gaze with cool challenge.

'No. Why?'

'Well—you—you're hardly dressed for—for what I had in mind.'

Oh, *why* had she said that? It gave him the perfect opening—one he took without hesitation.

'And what *did* you have in mind?'

'I told you! I thought we needed to talk!'

But now, of course, having put the suggestion into her own thoughts, she couldn't drag her wanton feelings back from the images they insisted on playing over and over in her mind.

The words 'hardly dressed' and 'half naked', when linked with Jake, did terrible things to her imagination, throwing up pictures of the time in his house in London and the way his body had looked out of his clothes. He had been all honed muscle and sleek power. The memory of the way that hard, warm chest had felt under her fingertips made it difficult to breathe with her heart beating fast high up in her chest. Her breasts tightened and ached and a slow coil of fire was awakening low down in her body, stirring, pulsing insistently.

'Yeah—you keep saying that—but you haven't yet said about what. And don't tell me again that I should put some clothes on—I'm perfectly decent for *talking*.'

The sarcastic emphasis he gave the word made it only too

plain that he was forcefully sceptical that it was really why she was here. The thought of what other interpretations he had put on her visit made her heart jerk uncomfortably and race even faster, painfully unevenly.

'And you're lucky I'm wearing this much. If you will come banging on people's doors at some ungodly hour, when most normal people are still asleep, then you have to take them as you find them. I don't happen to own a pair of pyjamas and—'

'Oh, did I get you out of bed?'

The thought of him in that bed, *without* pyjamas, was what pushed her into the stumbling question. That and the realisation that she had blundered in here without thinking of what he might have been doing. She had been so determined to see him, *needing* to see him, that she hadn't even thought that he might be asleep or…

'No, I wasn't asleep—and, before you ask the next question that is so clearly buzzing in your fertile little imagination, no, I was not with anyone else. There is no one in the apartment but you and me.'

She shouldn't feel relieved. There was no need for it. Jake Taverner meant nothing to her—*nothing*! But that didn't stop her shoulders from relaxing, or the breath that she had held in from escaping, making her realise very much too late how just the thought of the unspoken question had made her whole body tense—as if the answer to it had meant not nothing, but *everything*.

Now relief made her giddy and she couldn't hold back the bubble of laughter that escaped her.

'Do you realise that you've been clutching that coffee mug like a protective shield ever since I came in? Even when you folded your arms you still hung onto it.'

Taken unawares by the sudden change in her voice, Jake looked down at the mug in astonishment.

She was right. He had completely forgotten about the mug

in the moment that the ring of the doorbell had sounded through the flat, and he had been holding tight to it ever since.

But a protective shield?

That implied that he wanted her to come no closer and the exact opposite was true. What he wanted was her as close as she could possibly be. Intimately close, with their bodies joined…

Oh, hell!

Perhaps he *had* been using it as a defence against his own thoughts and feelings. With the mug in his hand he could hardly do what he most wanted to do—and that was to reach out, grab hold of the delicate shoulders under the loose pink tee shirt, and pull her close—

'Are you ever going to drink it?'

—and kiss those smiling—

Damnation. What had she said? Something about drinking.

'I think it's probably undrinkable.'

Another, clearer-minded glance down at the now-unpleasant-looking brown liquid had him grimacing in distaste.

'Totally disgusting. If you'll excuse me, I'll just get rid of it. Perhaps make another—would you like coffee?'

'That would be nice.'

Automatically she looked towards the kitchen door and he wondered if, like him, she was recalling the night in his house when, as he'd checked on the final preparations for the meal, she had wandered into the kitchen to join him.

He didn't want that happening this time.

'Go and sit down.'

He waved a hand towards the living room, not pausing to see if she followed his suggestion as he made his way into the kitchen, dumped the cold and unappealing contents of the mug down the sink, and forced his attention onto making some fresh.

It shouldn't have had the effect it did. He was in a kitchen, for heaven's sake. A sleek, modern kitchen full of stainless steel and slate and carefully planned spotlights. A practical room, an efficient room—perhaps a rather stark and functional room. But his thoughts were of sensuality and comfort, of softness and indulgence, as his imagination took over and took hold.

The metal finish of the kettle or the spoon in his hand felt like the warm silk of skin and hair. The scent of coffee grounds steeping in hot water evaporated, to be replaced by the heady perfume of roses and lily, mixed with warm, receptive, human skin.

Warm, receptive, *female* human skin.

'For God's sake, man! Pull yourself together!' he muttered angrily as the sound of the kettle, bubbling wildly, invaded his sensuous dream. He had left the lid off and it was now in danger of boiling dry. 'Get a grip.'

'What? Did you say something?'

'No!'

Too late. She had already appeared in the doorway.

'Do you need any help?'

'I told you to go and sit down.'

Wrong attitude. Wrong tone of voice. He could see the rebellion settling over her face, the spark of anger in her eyes.

'And who gave you the right to order me around? I don't take orders!'

'Yeah, I noticed.'

He drew in a deep, uneven breath, forced his mood back under control.

'What about requests?'

'What?'

Her half-smile was bemused, puzzled, a little shy. Hellishly cute.

He definitely wanted to see that smile again.

'You said you don't take orders—do you take requests?'

She was obviously intrigued now.

'I might.'

'Okay, then—Mercedes, *please* go and sit down.'

It worked. The smile was back. Wider and brighter than before. Wide enough to give him a sharp, painful kick of raw sensuality.

'Seeing as you asked so nicely...'

She was turning, preparing to do as he'd said, when the second brutal kick low down in his body made him wince inwardly.

'No! I mean...I changed my mind.'

This time she didn't speak, but directed a look of enquiry straight into his eyes.

Or was it enquiry? Was there a touch of challenge in there too?

'Don't go,' he said hoarsely, his lips and throat dry. 'Come here. *Please* come here.'

For a difficult second or two he thought she was going to refuse, but then she smiled again, more slowly this time, and turned back.

Each step seeming to take a lifetime, she walked deliberately towards him, her eyes locking with, and holding, his.

'You see how easy it is when you ask nicely,' she teased.

She was coming closer. So close that he could feel the warmth of her body reach out to touch him, the personal scent of her skin surround him like a cloud. The hunger for her was like a clawing need in the pit of his stomach, yearning, growing, demanding release.

'I'm sorry—I forgot my manners.' He had to fight to keep that hunger from showing in his voice. 'It won't happen again.'

Damn it, she had stopped just out of reach. Just too far away from him, so that it was impossible to touch her without making it look as if he was moving in on her and so giving her the chance to retreat fast. And if she did dodge away, then he doubted she would ever come close again.

But then of course there was that magic word.

'Please...'

He accompanied it with a careful crooking of one forefinger. Careful and slow, making no sudden movement that might make her startle like a wild deer wary of stepping into a trap. Her eyes were as wide and dark as the untamed creature, her head high, her movements cautious.

But she came closer. Close enough for him to touch a fingertip to her face just above her temple. To stroke it slowly—slowly—down her cheek and under her chin.

Watching the way that she couldn't stop her eyes from closing in instinctive sensual response, he took a step forward, closer, used the softest pressure of that single finger to lift her head, tilting her face towards his. Slowly. Carefully.

Now her mouth was his for the taking.

Another step forward.

Careful. Easy.

And he lowered his lips towards hers...

Mercedes couldn't believe she was doing this. She *shouldn't* be doing it. But she also knew that she couldn't resist. It was like being caught in an enchanter's spell; as if the delicate thread of magic that he had woven had been tossed over her head, around her, like some fragile but unbreakable lasso.

But deep down inside she knew that she didn't want to break free.

This wasn't like the hot and hungry, hurried, passionate grabbing and snatching need that had taken her in its grip that night in England. This was a slow and gentle, careful, easy enticement. It crept into her heart and mind, cajoling, persuading, tempting, and she couldn't resist it.

She didn't *want* to resist it.

When Jake smiled like that, he charmed his way into her

soul, which was where she knew he had always been right from the start, no matter how hard she had tried to persuade herself otherwise. And the murmured, 'Please…' had destroyed any hope she had had of holding out against him.

She might have been able to stand firm against Jake himself—but not the lethal combination of Jake's persuasive magnetism and her own yearning need. There was no resisting that. She might just as well run up the white flag right here and now and surrender completely.

And so she moved forward like someone hypnotised, in a trance.

His touch on her cheek had the same dreamlike effect. She barely felt its soft caress, but at the same time it made her close her eyes briefly in a reaction like that of a contented cat, responding to the most gentle of strokes.

This was what she wanted.

This and more.

And so when his strong finger moved under her jaw, lifting her chin, raising her face towards his, she went with it willingly. Her eyes locked with his so that she saw the way the blue deepened, darkening at the edges of the irises so that they looked almost all black. She read his intent in those eyes and was ready—waiting…willing.

The moment before his lips touched hers was like a lifetime. Her heart seemed to stand still; her breath caught in her throat and she thought that a few tiny seconds had never, ever felt so long—so unendurable.

It was as if everything were being played out in the slowest of slow motions.

But then his mouth took hers and her senses exploded, taking her thoughts with them. All she was aware of was the fierce, slow beginnings of the primitive burn of need starting up deep within her, and spreading like wildfire through the rest of her body, impossible to deny.

# CHAPTER ELEVEN

IT WAS the night in London all over again.

But this time Mercedes was expecting it, anticipating it—*wanting* it.

She wasn't unsure, and she wasn't apprehensive. She wasn't going to be shaken, right to the foundations of her soul, as she had been the first time, because she knew what was coming and longed for it. She was looking for that bolt of lightning, the electric shock, the searing heat that sizzled right through every nerve.

And she got it.

If possible, it was even wilder, even harsher, even more stunning than before. In a single, searing rush, her whole body became just one single blind, primitive gnawing sense of need. She was shaking with it, shivering in spite of the growing warmth of the day, her legs as weak and boneless as cotton wool beneath her.

'J-Jake…'

Even his name shook on her tongue as she tried to speak it. And her arms were equally unsteady as she reached up, fastened them around his neck, and clung. With their support she was able to stay upright enough to kiss him properly, to give him her mouth openly and fully as the pressure of his lips demanded.

The taste of him was like wine on her tongue, the scent of his body, clean and musky and intensely male, an added stimulus to her already throbbing senses, but, after having had to keep her distance for so long, it was touching him, knowing the feel of his skin warm and smooth as heated velvet under her hands, that finished her.

115

The hands that were looped around his neck were no longer still, no longer content to stay just as a support. She had to explore, tracing the long, powerful length of his back, feeling the taut muscles bunch and slide under her wandering fingers. She found the line of each rib, the indentation of his waist, the tight line of his spinal column. Her fingers tangled in the slippery sleekness of his hair, smoothed over the straight, strong shoulders, scraped against the night's growth of dark stubble on his cheeks and chin, the faint abrasion making her tingle wickedly.

And all the time Jake just held her. Held her tight and hard, crushed up close against him. Caught between the heat and power of his body, with the hardness of the worktop behind her digging into her back, Mercedes could not escape the hard, hot pressure of the forceful erection that swelled against the pit of her stomach, cradled in the curve of her pelvis.

The kisses that had started out rough and demanding and passionate now deepened, teased, tormented. Jake snatched tastes of her mouth, her skin; he kissed his way along the line of her jaw, nibbled at the soft lobe of her ear until she was moaning aloud in her need for more.

And he was there before her. Just as his wickedly tantalising mouth moved up and back towards her lips his even more knowing hands found their way under the loose folds of the bright pink tee shirt, and were inching upwards, slowly and deliberately.

Mercedes' breath caught in her throat and her tingling body was still, waiting—just waiting for the moment that those tormenting hands reached their goal and closed over her breasts. She wanted the feel of their heat and hardness on her sensitive flesh so much that it was an agony to wait. So much so that she could not hold back a protest when, unexpectedly, and very much unwanted, the movement slowed and stilled.

'No!' she groaned against the heat of his mouth. 'Oh, no!'
Jake's soft laughter was warm against her skin.

'Patience, *señorita*,' he reproved gently. 'Patience. We don't want to rush this, do we?'

'No—yes—no!'

Mercedes could only shake her head in confusion, not knowing what to say, how to answer him.

She wanted this—oh, *por Dios*, but she wanted it. She wanted to know it all, experience everything, and she wanted to take it slowly, indulge in every last sensation to the full. But at the same time she wanted to snatch at the feelings, grab them greedily and *know* them—now—fast—at once.

'Touch me, Jake,' she muttered, her mouth against the hard line of his jaw, rubbing her cheek against his, like a small, soft cat pleasure-marking a favourite spot. 'Really touch me—*please*.'

Jake's laughter was a warm, rich sound deep in his throat.

'So now you're the one saying please…and, like you, I respond so much better to a request.'

Before she had time to draw in another unsteady breath he had swung her off her feet and up into his arms. Shouldering his way out of the kitchen door, he carried her swiftly across the hallway and up the short flight of stairs. A bedroom door already stood open and just a few moments later he was lowering her onto the bed, tearing the loose pink tee shirt off as he did so.

'Touch you,' he muttered roughly, coming down beside her. 'Oh, yes, darling, I will touch you. But first we have to get rid of this…'

Strong, determined fingers dealt efficiently with the front opening of her bra, brushing the white silk aside and freeing the full curves of her breasts. Watching the intent look on his face, the darkened eyes as they feasted on the satin skin, the tightened nipples that he had exposed to his hungry gaze,

Mercedes held her breath, her stomach clenching sharply, waiting, aching, for the first, intimate contact.

The hand that had opened her bra lifted, tilted, moved slowly, deliberately, towards the right breast, and stopped, hovering just an inch away. So close that she could feel the heat radiating from it, but not feel it.

'Jake!' she protested weakly and saw his smile widen devilishly.

'Now, what was that word again?'

'Please...' It was just a whisper. 'Jake, please.'

Her breath stopped again as, with a dark, triumphant smile, he lowered his hand slowly, slowly, towards her hungry flesh.

But that was the last thing he did slowly. From the moment that his fingers touched her breast, the explosion of hot desire was nuclear. Mercedes jerked and shuddered under his caressing hand, his name a moaning sigh on her dry lips. Jake laughed softly, deep down in his throat, moving over her, covering her, the length and power of his legs nudging hers apart, coming to lie between them.

His hands were busy at the fastening of her jeans while his mouth worked a sinful magic on her breasts. Mercedes had never known that there were so many wild sensations possible as he kissed and licked and nipped softly at the delicate skin. But it was when that hot mouth closed over one distended nipple that she arched convulsively and cried aloud in her delight.

Two pairs of jeans were slipped off, thrown in a tangle on the floor. Jake wore nothing beneath his, but the tiny slip of silk that was all that was left on Mercedes' body might not have existed, providing no defence at all against those hard, determined hands, set on exploring every intimate inch of her.

Mercedes too wanted to know Jake, to feel him, to touch him, really touch him. Her movements were uncontrolled, jerky, almost frenzied as she tried to learn the different planes and shapes, the textures of his body. The straight, square power of his shoulders, the long sweep of his back. The hair-roughened chest and legs, the smooth, tight curves of his male buttocks. And there, at the very heart of his masculinity, the velvet and steel power of his erection.

Wonderingly her hands closed around him, tightened, smoothed.

'Mercedes...'

Jake's use of her name was both a protest and a sound of raw encouragement, but as she stroked along the length of him he jerked away, with a low, rough sound deep in his throat.

'No—enough—I won't be able to control myself.'

'Don't want control,' Mercedes muttered.

'No? Well, what do you want, sweetheart? This?'

His tongue encircled one taut nipple, tracing erotic trails round and round, before he took the straining tip hard into his mouth, laughing in triumphant delight as she writhed under the sensual torment.

'And what else? Here's something more you might want...'

Strong hands slid along the soft skin of her inner thighs, easing them apart, moving slowly, seductively, inescapably closer.

For long, unbearable seconds the hard fingers tangled in the dark curls shadowing her femininity, but then as Mercedes' head tossed frantically against the pillows in an agony of frustration he laughed again. Probed deeper, more intimately. His knowing touch found the hidden nub that was the trigger point of her most female pleasure and touched, stroked, aroused with practised skill. Driven beyond words, beyond thought, half blind with delight, Mercedes could only arch her body towards his touch, abandoning herself to the pleasure he was creating.

'Jake...Jake...'

His name was just a sigh of gratification on her parched dry lips and she reached for him, hands clutching, wanting to pull him closer to her—over her.

'Jake…'

But he resisted slightly, gently, but strongly enough to make her pause, open her eyes briefly, realising vaguely, with a sense not quite buried under the landslide of sensuality, just what he was doing.

This time the condoms were so much closer. In the drawer of the bedside cabinet, they needed no fetching, no interruption to their lovemaking, no breaking into the flow of heated passion.

And Mercedes was glad of that—so glad.

She wanted none of the time to think that had allowed the doubts and fears to whisper into her subconscious the last time. She didn't want to think or worry or care; she only wanted to feel and experience and *know*.

Know Jake as fully and completely as it was possible to know another human being. And to experience the fullest extent of his passion finally and totally.

Jake was sheathing himself in the condom and the wait was making her impatient. With a little moan she moved restlessly on the pillow, then froze as his hot, demanding mouth took her lips, her breast, subduing the protest before it had time to form.

'Not this time, my beauty,' he muttered thickly against her sensitised skin. 'You're not running away from me this time. This time you stay and see things through, my little tease. This time you get what you've been asking for.'

He couldn't believe she wanted to run away again!

Somehow the words registered through the burning haze that filled Mercedes' head, blurring thought, preventing speech. He couldn't think she didn't want this—that she was only teasing…leading him on…

It was the furthest thing from her mind.

She couldn't speak, couldn't find the words to tell him—but she could *show* him. Her body could speak for her. She could let him see how much she needed him, how much she *wanted* him.

Eyes closed, clutching at the hard shoulders above her, pulling him closer with all her strength, she writhed and arched, mutely inviting the intimate invasion she so longed for. And Jake was swift to respond.

With a raw, rough sound of triumph, he came over her once again, pushed his hands under her hips, cupping her buttocks as he lifted her towards him. The blunt heat of his sheathed penis probed the moist opening, slid deeper, then thrust in hard, taking full possession of her in a heartbeat.

And froze as the sudden swift, sharp pain made her gasp, her eyes opening wide and glazed in shock.

'Hell and damnation!'

Above her, Jake's dark face was still. His ice-blue eyes, clouded and blurred with shock, stared down into her stunned face, her widened eyes, in raw disbelief.

'Mercedes…' he grated, seeming to need to catch his breath. 'Sweetheart—beauty—is this—was this why…?'

Impatiently she shook her head, black hair flying out around her face as she moved in sharp denial. She didn't want to speak! Didn't want him to talk about something that was gone—over and done with.

Already the slight stinging pain was ebbing, fading as the renewed excitement, the pulsing need took over once again. There was some other sensation, unknown as yet, only just out of sight, one that her body yearned towards, needed so much. She couldn't bear it if it all ended now.

She could feel Jake's tension, sense his inclination to withdraw, to stop, and that was *not* what she wanted now. Not at all. Not now, not ever. If he stopped she felt that she would die of hunger, misery and bitter, cruel frustration.

'No,' she muttered thick and fast. 'Jake… No, no—no!'

And, matching the rhythm of her words with her body, she started to move herself, some female instinct as old as time teaching her just what to do, how to take Jake with her.

'Mercedes...' he tried again, but it was obvious from his tone that he was weakening.

Another provocative little twist of her body, a touch of her hands, and he flung back his head, his eyes closed tight, jaw set hard. Heat scored along the line of his cheeks as with a dark groan of surrender he abandoned himself to his body's need.

And he took Mercedes with him. With each thrust, each more powerful than before, he lifted her higher, further, closer and closer to that hidden, shimmering, tantalising goal.

Her heartbeat raced, her blood pounded, there was a fizzing mist before her eyes. She felt as if she were riding the highest, wildest, most magnificent wave she had ever seen, being lifted up and up, soaring, flying...until at last they reached the furthest, most brilliant, sun-sparkled peak and together tumbled over it into another world.

# CHAPTER TWELVE

THESE morning-after things were one hell of a lot easier to deal with if they actually happened the morning after, Jake thought reluctantly, raking his free hand roughly through his hair and staring straight up at the white painted ceiling, hunting for a way to broach the series of questions that was clouding up his mind.

If this had been the night time, the end of a long, busy day, and he and the woman he was with had had the sort of wild, abandoned sex that he had just experienced, then time and effort would take their toll. She—they—would inevitably fall asleep and stay that way until morning. The hours of darkness would slide away, providing a silent, hidden recovery time. A time of some adjustment and acceptance.

And so in the morning they would wake together, look at things in the cold light of day together. And together they would decide where they went from here.

But this was not one of those occasions.

For a start, the woman he had made love to had not been one of the sophisticated, knowing creatures he so often met in London and other cities of the world. She was Mercedes— Mercedes the treasured, indulged, adored only daughter of the Alcolar family. She was *Juan Alcolar's* child.

And she had been a virgin.

His restless, instinctive movement in reaction to that thought disturbed the woman at his side. Mercedes was lying with her head pillowed on his other arm and as it twitched involuntarily she stirred briefly, muttered something soft and low, then sighed deeply and drifted back into her dreams.

Jake's mouth twisted wryly at one corner. As he looked

down at her peacefully unconscious face it was so obvious
that nothing disturbed her sleep as she lay there. Whatever
dreams she was having, they were happy ones, tranquil ones.
Her expression was relaxed and totally serene, with even the
hint of a gentle smile to curve the corners of that luscious,
full, sexy mouth. The mouth he had kissed and caressed so
often in the past hour or more. The mouth that had opened
under his so willingly…so responsively…so enticingly.

But would she still be smiling when she woke up and
remembered?

When she realised what had happened?

'Mercedes?'

Even in his own mind he wasn't quite sure whether he
truly wanted to wake her or whether he pitched his voice at
a level somewhere between intrusive and barely audible so
as to salve his conscience but not to have any real effect.

They would have to talk eventually. But not yet. Not now.
Not until he had clear in his mind where they went from
here.

'Mercedes…'

'Mmm…'

Her only response was a deep, low sigh. A sleep-filled
sigh. He hadn't got through to her.

And perhaps that was just as well. He didn't trust himself
to speak to her if he had to right now.

Just who the devil was Mercedes Alcolar?

Was she the tease who had led him on, turned him on so
high that he had been screaming with it—then dumped him
flat and run out on him?

Or had she run out of sheer nerves because—as he had
found out today—that night would have been her first night
with any man?

But then again there was that other Mercedes—the one he
had encountered at Ramón's wedding, when she had claimed
not to know him at all. The one who was pure Alcolar from

the top of her shining black head to the smallest of her delicate pink toes. Icy cold, totally careless of other people's feelings and arrogant as hell.

That was the Mercedes who had issued the message her friend had passed on to him.

*She didn't want to waste any more of her time bothering with you.*

So if she didn't want to waste her time with him, then what the blazes was she doing in his bed right now?

Because one thing was sure—the time he had spent with her had most definitely not been wasted. With her he had just experienced the best, the most passionate, the most fulfilling sex he had ever had in his life, and it was something he wanted to repeat—again and again and again.

'Mercedes…'

It was getting late. The day was already hot, the sun high in the sky. She had arrived here so early that he doubted she'd had any chance to tell her father where she was going. If she was much longer, then she was going to have some serious explaining to do when she got back.

'Mercedes—time to wake up, baby.'

'Mmm?'

This time the sleepy mutter was more questioning and she stirred reluctantly, frowning and attempting to snuggle back down, bury her head in the soft pillows.

'Oh, no, you don't.'

Jake pulled his arm out from under her head, jolting her into further wakefulness.

'Come on, sleepyhead—the day started long ago.'

'Don't want to…' Mercedes muttered into the pillow, burrowing into the fine Egyptian cotton to get away from him.

But Jake was having none of that.

'Mercedes—Señorita Alcolar…'

He brought his face down close to hers, so that his cheek

almost rested on the soft hair, his mouth only an inch away from her rose-pink lips.

'Time to wake up and face reality.'

He saw the long, rich black lashes quiver, lift slightly, the gleam of her deep brown eyes watching him for a moment through the barely open slit.

'Jake…' She stretched his name into another long, drawn-out sigh.

'Yeah—'

His tolerance was drawn out way too far. He was rapidly losing patience. He wanted to know just what she was up to. Why she was here. What exactly was going through that complicated, confusing mind of hers?

'At least you remember who I am.'

That brought those dark eyes open wide, just for a second, but a moment later the heavy lids drooped back again, hiding their expression from him.

'Of course I remember,' she murmured, soft and low. 'How could I forget?'

Stirring again faintly, she reached out a hand, forefinger extended. Slowly and lightly she ran it down the side of his face, traced the outline of his mouth.

'You're the man I…'

That wandering finger froze and he could almost feel the sense of shock that rocketed through her. Her eyes remained closed but he suspected that behind the lowered lids she was suddenly wide awake—just not prepared to reveal her thoughts to him.

'You're the man who…'

With a sensuous little movement she wriggled near, sliding over the rumpled sheet so that the scent of her body rose from the warmth of the bed, setting his pulses throbbing in an instant.

'Mercedes.'

Jake tried to put a note of warning into his voice but either it hadn't worked or she totally ignored it because, still with her eyes closed, she came closer, reached out her arms, enclosed him in them. Her silky head lay against his naked chest and the warmth of her soft, curvy body was pressed along the hard length of his.

'You're *the man*...'

It was murmured huskily with her lips against his chest, the soft drift of her breath over his skin making him shudder, hardening him in an instant.

'We have to talk.'

'Later...'

Her hands were moving now, wandering softly all over his body, wickedly enticing, arousing, teasing. Taking his self-control with them and blowing his mind as they did so.

He had been trying to work out just which was the real, the true Mercedes Alcolar, and now, here, it seemed that he was being confronted by yet another one entirely. A woman whose seductive caresses and sultry kisses shattered his thought processes, driving all rational thought from his head in a heartbeat.

He felt the gentle heat of her touch on his back, smoothing over his buttocks, making his lower body clench convulsively. And all the time she pressed herself closer, her breasts crushed to his chest, the tiny curve of her soft belly against his, the cradle of her hips cushioning the hot force of the aching erection he couldn't control. And when her hands, deliberately provocative, moved in that direction, he could hold back no longer.

'Damn you, Mercedes...'

Twisting sharply, throwing her over onto her back, he covered her, kicking her legs aside, pushing his hungry body into her feminine warmth.

And she opened to him as if she had been made for him. She lifted her hips to him, welcoming him, encouraging him in the same moment that her lips clung to his, her tantalising tongue echoing the other, more intimate invasion in a way that drove him wild.

It was hard and hot, fast and furious. It was primitive and fierce, and so very basic in its ferocious yearning to appease the pounding demand of his senses. And Mercedes went with him every inch of the way, her body arcing to his, her hands clutching, her nails scoring small crescent marks into the tautly stretched skin of his back.

They reached the peak together, gasping their fulfilment into each other's mouths as wave after wave of ecstasy broke over them, reducing them to shuddering, exhausted wrecks. Totally spent, totally satiated, Jake collapsed on top of her, his chest heaving, his whole body limp. His ability to think obliterated.

*You're the man that I love. The man I adore.*

The phrases that had been inside her head when she'd wakened slid back into Mercedes' thoughts now, when she was too weak, too exhausted to keep them at bay.

*Jake Taverner, you're my love, my life, my heart, my soul—you're everything I want and all I ever dreamed of.*

It wasn't a decision she'd come to rationally, not a thought that she had worked out, worked through and seen it was the case. No, it had hit her like a blow between her eyes in the moment that, barely half awake, she had started to open her eyes and looked into the cool blue depths of Jake Taverner's watchful gaze.

'At least you remember who I am,' he had said, sounding gruff and remote and totally unloverlike. So very different from the man who had just made love to her so wonderfully.

'Of course I remember,' she'd replied. 'How could I forget?'

And in that instant it had hit her just what had happened.

Why she was here at all. Why she hadn't been able to stay away. Why Jake had been able to enchant her when she had thought that she had come here to negotiate an arrangement for his leaving.

She had fallen in love with him without knowing how or why or even when it had happened.

And she had almost let the secret escape her.

She had almost said, 'Of course I remember. You're the man I love.' But she had managed to catch the betraying words back in time—just. And then she had resorted to the ultimate in diversion techniques by seducing him so that he hadn't been able to think of anything else.

But that hadn't been the only reason she had had for enticing him into making love to her. Waking up slowly, reluctantly, from the dream she had been having, she hadn't wanted to open her eyes, hadn't wanted to return to cold reality at all.

She had been dreaming of Jake. Of his hard, warm body curled close to hers, the strength of his arms around her, the scent of his skin in her nostrils, the taste of him in her mouth. She had dreamed of his kisses, his caresses, his forceful, passionate lovemaking and the stunning, explosive heights to which it had taken her. The experience of the mind-blowing fulfilment she had never known before. And she hadn't wanted to leave that wonderful, delicious fantasy land.

But then she had woken and found that it was not the fantasy she thought. Jake was close by, his long body as naked as hers, his mouth kissably close. And the hunger had surged through her in an instant, stronger, fiercer than ever before because now she knew just what she wanted—and what she wanted was Jake and the rich, deep, stunning satisfaction that he could bring her.

Heaving a deep, deep sigh, Jake rolled away from her and lay on his back beside her, eyes closed, one arm flung up to cover and conceal them as well. *I'm not here,* his body language stated so clearly. Don't speak to me because I don't

want to talk. He might just as well have put up a sign—
'Keep out! Trespassers will be prosecuted!'

And she didn't have the courage to brave that silent barrier.
She suspected she knew what had put it there anyway in the
first place. Jake had had what he wanted from her; now he
wished she would just disappear. In fact, he would probably
have preferred it if she had got up and gone as soon as he
had made love to her earlier…

No!

Mercedes caught the thought back sharply before it had
any time to grow. Leaving it to develop would only allow
for the weak, foolish possibility that it had the right to exist.

Jake had not *made love* to her. Love didn't come into what
had happened between them. If she allowed herself to even
hope for that, then she was setting herself up for devastation
later when he made the truth plain to her. With her father's
example before her she would be a fool to think otherwise.
And—the thought drew a gasp of pain from her as memory
sliced into her mind reminding her, shockingly, unbelievably,
that she had forgotten completely about the beautiful blonde
she had seen letting herself into Jake's house on the night in
London.

That image was too sharp, too painful to cope with here
and now and in these circumstances. Perhaps if she put some
clothes on she would feel less devastated, less vulnerable.

Forcing herself upright, she tried to slide towards the edge
of the bed as unobtrusively as possible. Disturbing Jake
would result in the sort of repercussions she was really not
ready to face.

She was just about to get to her feet when his sudden
movement, flinging the concealing arm down to his side,
opening his eyes wide and staring at the ceiling, froze her
into shocked stillness.

'Well, my sweet Mercedes,' he said slowly, not looking at

her, not even the flick of an eyelid in her direction. 'Perhaps we'd better have that talk now.'

Did he know how much that 'my sweet Mercedes' hurt? Of course he did. That was why he had said it and why he had used that cynical, mocking voice deliberately aimed to mean exactly the opposite of the words.

'Wh—what talk?'

'The one you said you wanted,' Jake drawled, stretching indolently on the fine white sheets. 'The one you said you'd come here to have.'

He seemed totally unfazed in his nakedness, uninhibited and at ease, his relaxation setting Mercedes' teeth on edge.

She couldn't share in it, wishing desperately for something to cover her, but her clothes were scattered over the deep blue carpet, way out of her reach.

'That is why I came here!' she snapped.

'Oh, yeah?'

'Yes!'

She wished she hadn't glanced at him at just that moment because by doing so she caught the swift, cynical lift of one dark eyebrow, the coolly assessing gaze he slanted in her direction.

'I came here to talk to you,' she repeated with sharp emphasis.

'So you did.'

The cynical tone and the faint, knowing smile were just too much.

'All right—don't believe me. I don't care what you think.'

'You don't know what I think,' Jake said, his tone darkening ominously. 'So don't jump to conclusions. You said you came here to talk—to see if we could come to some sort of arrangement. So exactly what sort of *arrangement* did you have in mind?'

What sort of arrangement?

Memories of the thoughts that had been in her mind as she

had been driving here—had it really been just a couple of hours ago?—floated around inside Mercedes' head. She had been so sure then of what she'd felt, what she'd wanted to say. She remembered repeating phrases over and over to herself as she had marched up the stone steps to the door of the apartment building, travelling up to this floor in the lift. But those thoughts were broken now and disjointed, brief snatches of ideas coming to the surface and then disappearing again before she could grasp them, turn them into any coherent argument. She couldn't find the mental strength to string two rational thoughts together.

And what made things so much worse was the appalling vulnerability she felt just sitting here—on the bed where they had just had the most passionate, heartbreakingly wonderful sex. Sitting here and knowing that while she was still drifting in the ecstatic aftermath of the delirium of pleasure that had taken her apart, *he* had been coolly thinking back over the time when she had arrived, remembering the 'arrangement' she had said they needed and was now prepared to discuss it quite coldly and rationally. It was as if their lovemaking had never been.

Which, of course, for him it hadn't, she reminded herself, the taste of bitter misery acid in her mouth. Once again she had fallen into the cruel trap of calling what had happened between them *lovemaking* when for Jake it had been nothing but some self-indulgent sexual gratification. A passing pleasure that was over now and done with—as transient as a good meal or a glass of fine wine.

'Don't you think you might at least have the courtesy to let me get dressed before we have this conversation?' she flung at him, hiding the burn of pain behind a mask of anger.

It didn't seem to affect him in the slightest, bouncing off his impenetrable indifference without seeming to leave a mark.

'It's a little too late for false modesty,' he commented cynically. 'We've got way past that.'

The burning scrutiny of his cold, pale eyes seemed to sear over her exposed skin with an icy contempt, making her want to snatch at the nearest sheet and pull it up close around her for protection. Only knowing the way he would interpret that as having her on the run, so to speak, hiding from his scorn and showing how badly rattled she was, made her change her mind and force herself to stay where she was, enduring his disparaging stare.

'Well, you may be capable of discussing things while stark naked—but I'm afraid I prefer to get dressed. In fact...'

She allowed herself to add a small, expressive shudder that was partly real but mostly faked. It came from a defensive need to let him know he wasn't the only one who could switch off the wild passion they had shared and change to cool-minded control in the space of a heartbeat. So what if it showed on the outside but had no effect internally at all?

'I'd really like to have a shower.'

'Be my guest.' Jake matched her lack of concern and outstripped it without any effort. 'The bathroom's—'

'I know where it is,' Mercedes cut him off short. 'This is my brother's apartment, after all. You're more of a visitor here than I am.'

And that put him in his place, Jake reflected as she stalked past him, head high and proud, snatching up her clothes, heading for the bathroom door. *She* belonged here; he did not. *She* was the Alcolar while he was just some foreign nobody. Someone good enough for a quick tumble in bed when the need took her, but nothing more.

In fact, her fastidious little shudder had said, she couldn't wait to shower—to wash off the contamination of his touch.

He had come here resolved to put the damn ancient feud behind them—leave it back in history where it belonged. But it seemed that, with every action she made, Mercedes was determined to prove that the Alcolar arrogance was alive and thriving.

Well, if that was the way she wanted to play it, then he would match her step for step.

# CHAPTER THIRTEEN

IT WAS one thing deciding to play this the way Mercedes wanted it—the Alcolar way—Jake told himself half an hour later. But it was quite another to make himself stick to that decision in reality.

Because reality was Mercedes appearing out of the shower looking so unlike herself that for a moment or two he almost believed she were someone else.

With her long black hair soaked through and lying flat and dripping around her shoulders, her oval face scrubbed clean, pink and glowing with nothing more than the natural colour brought to her cheeks by the warmth of the shower, she looked like a small child on her way to bed. The towelling robe—Ramón's towelling robe—that she had obviously found hanging on the back of the bathroom door was wrapped practically twice around her slender waist and pulled tight, and still totally swamped her fine-boned body, only adding to that impression of a little girl lost.

It was only when he looked into her face and saw the stormy, mutinous look in her eyes, the stiff, haughty set of her features, the defiantly lifted chin and unsmiling mouth, that he recognised the other Mercedes—the one who could turn on him a look that would transform lesser men into a heap of ashes at her feet, quelling them with a glance.

But today there was something different about even that expression—the one he had come to call the Alcolar look. Today that defiance had a touch of bravado about it that he had never noticed before. The neat chin was held perhaps just an inch or two too high, the tight mouth could be clamped in a line of nervousness rather than pride and the whole effect was of someone at war with herself—determined not to show the unease she was feeling.

And seeing that, and remembering the discovery he had made—that she was a virgin, had been a virgin—he reined in the biting remark that was on the tip of his tongue and instead pitched his voice at a lower, more neutral level.

'I thought you were getting dressed,' he said carefully.

He'd taken the opportunity of her absence to shower in the *en suite* bathroom of one of the apartment's other bedrooms and was now dressed again in the comfortable jeans he'd had on when she'd arrived, but this time with a fresh white polo shirt worn loose over the waistband of his trousers.

'Something wrong with your clothes?'

'My—the tee shirt got ripped.' It clearly stuck in her throat to say that. 'It's unwearable.'

'Well, you can't go home like that.'

Jake sipped the glass of iced water he'd poured for himself. 'Whatever would *Papá* think?'

That earned him the sort of glare he expected so that he had to take another hasty swallow of his drink to hide the smile.

She might think that she looked fierce and furious but the reality was that like this, with the robe falling down almost to her ankles, and the sleeves gaping widely around her narrow wrists, she looked drowned and reduced by its size. In fact, with her hair drying into a soft, black halo around her scrubbed face, she looked like nothing so much as a small, fluffy black kitten that had fallen into the bath and come up spitting and hissing ineffectually at the world. It was that thought that made him take pity on her.

'There must be a tee shirt or something in Ramón's room that will do. Why don't you help yourself?'

'Of course…'

The sudden relaxation of the tension in her shoulders told

him without words that she hadn't thought of her brother's clothes. That she had been nerving herself to ask him for something of his to wear and hating the idea of it.

Which brought a strange and difficult conflict of feeling along with the realisation. What was he to this woman that she could sleep with him—share her body with him in the most intimate act that a man and woman could share—and yet the idea of wearing his clothes, even clothes that were freshly washed and hadn't touched his skin in days, made her turn pale at the thought?

'Help yourself.'

He kept it casual with a struggle, fighting to swallow down the biting comments that demanded release as he saw the obvious relief on her face, the way she hurried to his cousin's bedroom as if she couldn't wait. But the anger still surfaced when she came back, wearing a loose navy blue tee shirt she had found in one of the cupboards.

It covered her almost to her thighs, the sleeves falling half-way down her arms, and so, with the denim jeans underneath, there wasn't really very much of her showing apart from the small bare feet that padded on the polished wooden floor. But the way that she kept tugging it down as far as it could go set his teeth on edge with the unspoken implications of her actions.

'So are you ready to talk now?' he enquired, seeing her wince at the biting edge to his tongue. 'Do you feel respectable enough to discuss things?'

'I'm fine, thank you.' She was back to being stiltedly formal, clearly desperate to put some distance between them.

'Are you sure? Or is there some other part of your body that you would like to cover—your toes, perhaps? Would you like to borrow some socks as well?'

'Don't be ridiculous! There's no need for that!'

'No? I wouldn't want you to think that I might be tempted

to pounce on you just because you'd left an inch or two of flesh exposed.'

'That isn't what I was thinking!'

The blank, stunned look she turned on him told him even more than her words that his thoughts were off beam.

'No?'

'No, of course not! I just—you wanted to talk,' she finished abruptly, going to one of the big caramel-coloured armchairs and sitting down in it, curling her feet up on the soft leather seat. 'So let's talk. Say what you have to say.'

*And then I can go home.*

She didn't say the words. She didn't have to. They were written all over her face. But like him she had obviously decided that discretion was the better part of valour and she was determinedly keeping to the least contentious topics possible, holding back the subjects that might cause trouble.

'It's more what *you* wanted to say…'

He wished he'd never said that about her toes. Now as he sat there all he could think about was how small and enticing those small, slender feet looked, curled up, tucked under her tight little bottom. The toes were peeping out long and slender, tipped with nails painted a bright, pearlised pink, and he had to swallow hard to fight down an unnerving need to kneel beside her and press his mouth to their tender softness.

'You came here to discuss some sort of arrangement,' he explained when she looked bewildered. 'At least, that's why you said you were here.'

'Well, I didn't just turn up at the flat wanting to go to bed with you!' Mercedes flashed at him. 'That couldn't have been further from my mind!'

How did he manage to do that? she wondered as he just looked at her, without saying a single word. How did he manage to put doubt, scepticism and frank disbelief into just a single look from those cool, disturbing eyes, so that she felt as small as an insect crawling over the floor—and just as unimportant, easily crushed underfoot.

'If you say so,' he murmured.

It was the last straw. Ever since she'd arrived at the apartment nothing had gone the way she'd planned it. It seemed that no matter which way she turned this man was there, blocking her way, thwarting her every plan, taking every action and twisting it into some motivation that she couldn't recognise. Ever since she had met Jake Taverner at the damn party in London it seemed that her life just hadn't been her own and she desperately wanted it back again.

'I've had enough!' she exploded. 'More than enough! I don't have to stay here and listen to this—I'm going home!'

She had stormed to her feet, was marching towards the door, when a cool, collected voice behind her brought her up sharp.

'Running away again, Señorita Alcolar?' Jake asked quietly, but the bite of cynicism was there in his tone, stinging like the flick of a cruel leather whip. 'When are you going to stay and face—?'

'I am *not* running anywhere!'

Mercedes whirled to face him, glaring her anger into his infuriatingly calm, set face. Above the unyielding line of his mouth, the steel-blue eyes were alert and watchful, noting every play of emotion across her face, every small change of expression, so that she felt that the insect he had reduced her to was now being coldly and analytically dissected and viewed under a microscope.

'I am not running anywhere,' she repeated with fierce emphasis. 'And definitely not *again*.'

'No? So what about that night in London? You definitely hightailed it out of there as fast as you could, without so much as a goodbye.'

Suddenly, disturbingly, his expression changed. His eyes

darkened, the cold, straight line of his mouth eased and she watched him uncoil his long body from where he was sitting and get to his feet.

'Mercedes—you should have said. If it was the fact that you were a virgin that scared you...'

'Oh, yes, sure—and you would have stopped right then and there and said, Never mind, my dear, I can—'

'I might have done!'

It was a lion's roar, the roar of a true dominant male, kicked just where it hurt him most—in his pride.

'I bloody well would have done—if you'd given me a chance!'

He was coming towards her now, face set in brutal lines of anger. Anger that etched white marks around his nose and mouth, set his jaw like rock.

'And did you give me that chance, Señorita Alcolar? Well, *did* you?'

'N-no.'

Mercedes forced herself to hold her ground in spite of the near-desperate need to take several hasty steps backwards, get as far away from him as she possibly could.

'No.'

To her relief he came to a halt on the single word. Stopping a few metres away from her, he just looked into her face.

'No,' he said again. 'You didn't even stay around to find out what I'd say—or think. You were gone before I realised it.'

'Just as well, don't you think?' Mercedes tossed at him, hating the way that *he* could make *her* feel guilty when she had been the one who had been conned and taken for a ride. The one who was being used in all this.

'Just as well...?'

Jake became totally still, frowning as he considered this

last accusation. The darkness in his eyes disturbed her. He genuinely seemed not to know what she was talking about.

'And what does that mean?' he demanded.

'That it could have proved awkward if I'd stayed around and still been there when your girlfriend got home!'

Oh, damn, damn, damn!

She'd sworn that she would never, ever mention that. That she would rather die than let him know she realised just how badly he had used and humiliated her that night. She had never wanted him to know, because that would mean he would also know that she had come crawling back—that she hadn't really been able to get away. Until the realisation that she had been deceived had broken her totally.

As a result, she'd been such a wreck by the time she'd got back to the flat that Antonia had simply taken charge. Antonia had taken the phone call that Jake had had the nerve to make, pretending concern. And Antonia had dealt with him, sending him away with a stinging flea in his ear, when he had called at the flat the next day on some pretext. Mercedes had been too upset even to face him.

'My girlfriend—do you mean Karen?'

'I don't know her name, but know what she looks like—tall…'

'Platinum-blonde—almost-white hair.' Jake took up the description with a readiness that made her stomach heave nauseously.

Even now, poor stupid, gullible fool that she was, she had allowed herself to hang onto a tiny, sneaking hope that maybe, just maybe, this Karen had not been who she'd thought she was. That she had not been there for Jake but for…

For what? She didn't know and she didn't care. She had only hoped—and been desperately disappointed.

'Hair cut very short—almost cropped, and very slim…'

'And she has a key to your front door, and uses it as if it was her own home.'

She didn't want to remember but she couldn't help it. In her mind she was back in London, in the dark, wet night, standing shivering, watching the tall blonde walk up the steps to the door, insert her key in the lock…hearing her call out…

'She *had* a key to my house,' Jake put in sharply. 'I thought I'd got it back from her. Obviously I hadn't counted on her having a copy made.'

Mercedes spared him just one vicious, fulminating glare. He could have come up with something better than that! Something that could at least have had a chance of convincing her. Something that…

Oh, dear God! She realised just what she had been thinking.

*Something that could at least have had a chance of convincing her.* She had actually hoped he could persuade her that this Karen's appearance had been totally innocent. That he had not been expecting her—that she was nothing to him.

And she, Mercedes, weak, blind, besotted fool that she was, had *wanted* to believe him!

Unable to bear to look at him any more, unable even to stay in the same room as him, she spun away wretchedly, snatching up her bag and heading for the door as fast as she could go. She knew what she expected; she'd even nerved herself for it, her shoulders hunched against the accusation of running away again that she expected he would toss after her like a casual blow.

Surprisingly it didn't come. Instead there was just a single word—her name.

'Mercedes…'

Let her go, you fool! Jake told himself furiously. Let her go and get your life back—your sanity.

He'd never run after a woman in his life and he didn't intend to start now. In fact, he'd never reacted to any woman

in the way that he'd responded to Mercedes Alcolar. Since
he'd met her, his whole life had been off balance. She had
become an obsession with him, a passion that he couldn't rid
himself of.

If he hadn't known that she was inevitably going to be at
Ramón's wedding, then he would have wasted his time and
his energy hunting her down, finding out where she lived and
coming to find her. He wouldn't have been able to get her
out of his mind if he hadn't. He'd known he had to see her
just one more time.

*No, admit it, you fool, that just isn't true!*

Seeing her just one more time would never, ever have been
enough. He had known from the start that he'd had to get
her into his bed. That he wouldn't be able to rest until he'd
known the full sexual satisfaction he had sensed instinctively
that this woman could bring him. If he didn't, then he'd suspected that he would be hungry for life.

And it had been every bit as good as he had dreamed—
better than he could have imagined. But if he had hoped that
satisfying the desire to make love to her would appease the
demanding hunger that had eaten at him ever since that first
meeting, then he couldn't have been more wrong.

The truth was that it had made it all the worse.

He still wanted her.

More than wanted her. His body ached to see her walk
away from him, his lips hungered for the taste of her sweet,
soft skin against them, his mind refused to let go of the memory of how it had felt to have her naked and willing—oh, so
willing!—underneath him.

That knowledge hadn't appeased anything. Instead it had
fed his need for her, making it spiral out of control so that
he couldn't stand by and watch her walk out of the room and
out of his life.

If he let her go now, then he knew that he would never
get her out of his mind ever again. She would always be

there in his thoughts, as she had been these past weeks, driving sleep away, keeping him restless and sweating all night long. And if he managed to sleep at all then she haunted his dreams, tormenting and tantalising him until he woke aching with need and shaking in frustration.

Did he want to go back to that?

Did he hell!

She hadn't responded to his use of her name. Hadn't even reacted or glanced at him when he'd spoken. Doggedly she kept on going, not looking back; not looking anywhere but at the door.

And if she went out that door he would lose her for good, he was sure of it.

It was decision time. Now or never.

He launched himself after her, reaching out to grab her arm.

'Mercedes—no!'

She didn't know he had come up behind her until he caught hold of her, jerking her to a stop and whirling her round to face him.

This close, he seemed taller than ever. Taller, darker, stronger, more dangerous. His chest was just a solid, powerful wall, and she forced herself to try and focus on one of the three buttons at the neckline of his shirt. She couldn't look up into his face—wouldn't look up. If she did then he would see the way that her eyes were still swimming with tears and that would be the final, the ultimate humiliation.

'Are you going to do it again?' he demanded, low and fierce and harsh.

That brought her head up sharply, and she blinked frantically to clear the moisture from her eyes before he caught sight of it.

'Do what again?'

She tried to sound cold and indifferent but only succeeded

in sounding tart and belligerent, her voice cracking betrayingly in the middle.

'Run out on me without giving me a chance to say anything—to explain.'

'And you have an explanation?'

'Yes, I have one.'

It was a cold, blank statement.

'But only if you'll do me the courtesy of listening.'

She didn't want it to, but something in his voice, in his face, got through to her.

More than that, the way that he phrased what he said, and the note of something close to aggression in his voice, made it impossible for her to move any further.

He wasn't going to protest his innocence; he wasn't pushing an explanation at her, forcing it on her, to defend himself. Instead, he was stating, coldly and bluntly, that he wasn't going to speak unless she wanted him to.

And did she *want* him to?

Mercedes couldn't find an answer to that question and the struggle to find one, but not to show just how much the question meant to her in the first place, tensed every muscle in her body, especially the ones in her face. She could feel her jaw tightening, her mouth compressing, and the fight against the tears that still threatened at the back of her eyes meant that she could only stare at him with a wide, emotionless gaze, knowing her lack of expression must look mutinous and defiant.

'Okay.'

Abruptly Jake released her, letting her arms drop to her sides with a jolt. Silent and sober-faced, he moved past her, opening the door—opening it wide.

'I'd prefer it if you left now. And don't come back.'

The words seemed to hit like blows in the face. Mercedes flinched inwardly, sharply, unable to believe how much they had hurt.

How could anything hurt any more? And how—*how*—could this hurt more than ever before? She had known that he had lied to her, that he had been playing her along and using her when they had been together in London. So why should she now find that his lack of interest in explaining affected her more than that knowledge?

She took a couple of steps towards the door, her eyes on Jake's face all the time. He simply watched her, his handsome features set into a stony mask of blank indifference, not a muscle moving. But there was something about his eyes that caught and held her transfixed. Her footsteps froze and she could only stand motionless and unsure, not knowing whether to go or stay.

'Wh—what do I say to my father?' she managed to croak, her voice dry and rusty as if it hadn't been used for months.

'I'm sure you'll think of something.'

The steel-blue gaze turned pointedly towards the door and then back again and she tried to force her feet to move—and failed.

'All right—so explain.'

If she'd expected relief, or even satisfaction, to show on his face, there was nothing. He simply looked her straight in the eye, clear blue locking with clouded, uncertain brown and not flickering, not hesitating.

'Karen and I were a casual thing. At least I thought it was casual. She obviously didn't. I had told her it was over some days before and I asked for my key back then. She gave it to me—or, at least, I thought she did. I had no idea that she had an extra key made. And I certainly had no idea that she was going to waltz back into my life that night as if nothing had happened.'

His scowl was dark enough to be convincing. And the way that he spoke of this Karen made it clear that there was no affection there for her. At least not now.

But was it enough?

She was desperately afraid that she was persuading herself to believe what she so wanted to believe.

'She was away on a modelling job and she got back a day early. She thought that she'd given me long enough to come to my senses—she couldn't have been more wrong.'

Something in her face had given away what she was thinking. He had moved away from the door as he spoke, giving it a small kick so that it swung partially closed. Not slamming it totally shut in a way that showed how confident he was that he had won—but just enough to make it obvious he knew the way her mind was working.

'What I want to know is how you even knew anything about Karen in the first place. I thought you'd run out on me.'

'I did.'

She didn't want to tell him because it meant admitting the truth, and the truth was that she had never been able to break free from him, not properly. And letting him know just how much she was in his power was dangerous; really dangerous.

'Then how…?'

'I came back.'

It was just a whisper, low and shaking so that he must have had to strain to hear it. But he caught it and nodded his dark head slowly.

'You came back,' he echoed on a note that was like a tiger's cruel purr, rich and dark with savage satisfaction. 'You ran out on me but you came back.'

'It was l-like you said—I was scared. I panicked and I ran. And then…'

But she couldn't admit to the rest. Couldn't detail how she had come crawling back, unable to get away from the sensual spell he had tangled her in.

'I came back and I saw K-Karen arrive and get out of her car. She had a key. I saw her go in…'

'And if you'd just stuck around a minute or two longer

then you'd have seen her come right out again,' Jake declared bluntly.

In his thoughts he was reliving the moment that he had heard the door open: how he had thought it was Mercedes coming back—the disappointment when he had realised it was Karen.

He hadn't been at all polite, he recalled ruefully. He hadn't even tried to be gentle. But then he hadn't *felt* very gentle. His still aroused body had been clamouring for satisfaction— and even then he had known that it wasn't a satisfaction that Karen could have given him. It was Mercedes he'd wanted. Mercedes he'd ached for.

He might have pulled on his clothes, but he'd still felt as naked and as raw as the moment that he had gone back to the bedroom and found that she was gone. That she had disappeared, leaving no sign, no trace of the fact that she had even been there.

He had been heading for the door to go after her; to try and hunt for her in the dark, rain-slicked streets, when he had heard the key in the lock and Karen's voice calling his name.

'I gave her just long enough to hand over her copy of the key and then I made sure she left.'

Mercedes looked stunned—or was it relief that played across her delicate features? And suddenly he was looking at that night—and its repercussions—in a very different way. A way that made the stingingly insulting message her friend had relayed to him not the deliberately contemptuous put-down he had believed it, but the hurt response of a woman— a virgin—who thought she had been used and wanted to lash out.

'I told her not to come back. I went out to look for you but you'd disappeared.'

'But—but—why?'

'Why?'

Jake expelled his breath on a deep, uneven sigh, raking one hand roughly through the thick darkness of his hair.

'Mercedes, don't you listen to a word I say? I told you—I want you and only you. I can't get enough of you. That's why I don't want you to go.'

'You really don't...'

Her eyes were wide, luminous in the glow of the sun through the huge, uncurtained window.

'I really don't.'

He took a risk, stepping forward, coming closer, and to his relief she didn't flinch or turn, making no move to get away.

'I want you to stay because I want to do this...'

Slowly he reached out and stroked a hand over the silken length of her jet-black hair, now almost totally dry and falling like a soft cloud halfway down her back.

She shivered underneath his touch but she didn't resist and she stood still, quivering like a nervous, half-tamed thoroughbred that knew the touch of her master even though she hadn't yet come to fully accept it.

'And I want to do this...'

The caressing hand moved upwards, over her shoulder, the long, slender line of her neck. It stroked her cheek, her jaw, sliding under the fine bone and lifting her face towards his.

'And this...'

A kiss. A slow, long, lingering kiss that started gentle and, taking its time, grew stronger second by second, adding passion to gentleness, demand to passion until her mouth opened under his.

Her lips parted on a sigh and the tender touch of her tongue on his sparked a rush of hot desire all over again.

She was in his arms, held close, held tight, being kissed and kissing him back.

But a moment later that kissing was just not enough. In the same moment they acted, snatching at the fastenings of their clothing, pulling, tugging, their breath coming raw and ragged.

Their clothes fell on the floor and they fell on top of them, reaching for each other, stroking, touching, clutching...

Hungry. Needing. *Wanting.*

Wanting so much that it was like a tidal wave breaking over their heads, swamping them, drowning them, carrying them away on a hot, golden flood of sensation. Taking them higher and higher and higher until once more the tension was too much to bear, blazing so bright that inevitably it splintered, shattering into a myriad multicoloured fragments that showered down around them, taking their consciousness with it.

It was a long, long time before either of them stirred. Before Jake could even move or think or do anything but feel.

But at last he rolled away from her, lying back once more, his broad chest heaving, snatching in deep raw breaths as he struggled to get his heart to slow enough so that he could speak.

'Oh, Mercedes—my dear Señorita Alcolar. Now we really do have a reason to pretend to be engaged. What do you think your loving *papá* would think if he knew what had happened here today?

# CHAPTER FOURTEEN

'Now *we really do have a reason to pretend to be engaged.*'

Mercedes wished that she could get those words out of her thoughts. She wished that she had never heard them or at least that, having heard them, she could erase them completely from her memory. But she had heard them, and she couldn't forget them.

What she could do was to try not to think of them, and that was something she had resolved to do. It might be weak, it was most probably foolish, it was definitely dodging the issue, but it was the only way she could handle it and get any happiness from the situation.

Because she was determined to snatch at some happiness.

Knowing that she had fallen deeply in love with Jake, she wanted as much time as she could have with him—under any conditions. She wouldn't ask for him to love her—she knew that was just a dream, like asking for the moon. He had never spoken a word of love or anything remotely like it. But at least he felt the fierce, overwhelming physical passion for her that he had shown over and over again when she had visited him in Ramón's apartment. That was something that would hold him close to her for as long as it lasted.

And he clearly did plan to stay for some time. Why else would he say that they should continue with their make-believe engagement?

It couldn't be just to please her father, because she knew Jake Taverner well enough to realise that he didn't do anything to please other people unless it pleased him as well. So if it pleased him to stay, then he would stay and she would go along with what he wanted if it meant having him near for as long as she could.

Soon enough he would leave, go back to England, and maybe for a while he would accept a long-distance relationship, but she had no hope that Jake would tolerate that for long. Inevitably he would grow tired of it and then they would go through the pretence of falling out, breaking up, and she would have to face the anguish that losing him would bring.

But for now he was here. And she would try to make that enough for as long as it lasted. Though there were times when the knowledge that nothing was as her family believed it to be—or as she longed for it to be—was almost more than she could bear.

The day that Jake had brought up the question of a ring had been one of those.

'Perhaps we should choose a ring,' he had suggested one day when they had spent the morning exploring Barcelona and were relaxing over coffee in a small café.

'A ring?'

For a couple of seconds Mercedes didn't register just what he meant and could only stare at him blankly, frowning her confusion.

'What sort of a ring?'

'An engagement ring,' Jake explained with no noticeable sort of emotion in tone, nothing to give her any idea how to play this. 'What else?'

'Why would I want an engagement ring?'

She couldn't help herself; the words just slipped out, pushed out by her inner thoughts, the ones she didn't dare to let him suspect. Why would he think that she should want a ring to mark a relationship that didn't even exist?

'It is normal for engaged couples.'

'But we're not exactly a *normal* engaged couple. In fact we're not even engaged—as you know only too well.'

The look he slanted at her from those ice-blue eyes made her shiver in spite of the midday heat.

'But we need to keep up appearances if this engagement is to be believed.'

'Why should I care about keeping up appearances?'

'I thought that was exactly what you—and your *papá* were most concerned about.'

There was a definite edge to his voice now, and if possible his eyes had grown colder than ever.

'It's only because he already believed that we...' she managed, the words wooden and stiff on her frozen tongue. 'Because you led him to believe that we were already lovers.'

'And he was none too pleased to think it.'

Jake appeared to be focusing his attention on stirring his coffee, staring down into the cup as he did so. But Mercedes had the distinct impression that his concentration was firmly fixed on her voice and her slightest reaction.

'He seemed to think you'd let the family down,' he murmured cynically.

'This is Spain, not England,' Mercedes reminded him tartly. 'And in my father's opinion a respectable young woman doesn't...doesn't...'

'Doesn't throw herself at a man and just leap into his bed?'

'I didn't throw myself at you!' she protested sharply.

'I didn't see you fighting me off either. And that night in London, I definitely got the impression that you were making some of the running—if not most of it.'

Mercedes felt her cheeks colour fierily and her hand shook so much that she had to slam her cup back down into its saucer for fear of slopping coffee all over the polished wood of the table.

'I—I'd had a bit to drink.'

'No, you hadn't,' Jake shot back, his glittering gaze flicking up at her face, just once, then dropping down again. 'I know because I poured every drop that went into your glass. You were no more drunk than I was.'

'I...'

Mercedes tried to answer him but her voice failed her miserably. What *could* she say? How did she explain her behaviour when it hadn't even been understandable to herself?

At least not then. Now of course she saw what had been happening to her only too well. She had been in the first stages of a major infatuation—an infatuation that had turned out to be the precursor of a life-changing experience.

She had taken the first steps towards falling in love with Jake Taverner.

But she couldn't admit that, not to a man who had just offered her an engagement ring—a *fake* engagement ring— with as little concern as if he had been suggesting she wear a trinket from a cheap market stall.

'I wasn't thinking clearly.'

She hadn't been thinking at all, but that was something else she wasn't prepared to admit.

'And were you still not thinking straight when you ran?'

It was a question that had been fretting at his mind ever since that night, Jake admitted to himself. One that he really needed an answer to.

He didn't like the idea that, unaware of the fact that she had been a virgin, he might have been rough or inconsiderate and so sent her flying out of the house in a panic.

Mercedes picked up her spoon, looked as if she was going to put it into her coffee and stir the life out of it. But then, abruptly, she clearly changed her mind and let it drop back into the saucer with a sharp clatter.

'I don't think I was thinking at all then.'

Which was no answer at all. And it forced him into asking the question he had wished he could avoid.

'Did I frighten you?'

'Frighten me?'

That brought those big, deep brown eyes up in a rush to stare into his face in a sort of shocked bewilderment. The bewilderment was some sort of a relief, but the shock twisted uncomfortably in an already uneasy conscience, making him clench his hands around his coffee-cup until his knuckles showed white.

'No…'

The rush of relief as she shook her head was like a blow in his face, so fierce that for a moment his vision blurred as he watched the way her black hair swung around her shoulders with the movement.

'I frightened myself,' she added unexpectedly.

'What?'

It was the last thing he had been expecting and it confused him even more.

'I frightened myself—because I jumped in with both feet.'

Seeing his frown, she sighed faintly.

'This is embarrassing. You know about my father's past history—and the way I have a brother and two half-brothers.'

'And Ramón and Alex both have different mothers.'

Jake fought to keep his tone noncommittal. Now was not the time for her to learn that he knew more about her family situation than she had ever realised. Perhaps, if he played his cards right, she need never know. What was the point in upsetting things by telling her now? She would probably walk out on him if he did.

She was going to walk out on him anyway, one day, inevitably. Neither of them had offered any sort of commitment to this relationship, and certainly Mercedes had shown no sign of wanting anything more. But there was no need to push her into leaving before the passion between them wore itself out. There was still plenty there that he wanted to hold onto—for as long as she would let him.

'So how did you feel when these guys suddenly turned up out of the blue and announced that you were related?'

How had she felt when her father had proved himself a womanising rat, who hadn't been able to stay faithful to one woman in his life?

The look she turned on him was sharp, stricken, and he felt that he had somehow, inadvertently, put his finger on a painful memory for her. It wasn't a comfortable feeling and it rocked once again his mother's conviction that Mercedes was an Alcolar through and through, cold and arrogant as her father.

'It must have been a facer.'

'That's an understatement.'

She shivered faintly, just remembering.

'Ramón was totally up front about it all. He just marched into my father's office, demanded to know the truth—and wouldn't leave until he got an answer. With—with Alex, it was different...'

Her voice faltered, died away.

'How different?' Jake enquired when she had been silent for several moments, staring down into her almost empty coffee-cup. 'What happened?'

'He didn't let anyone know he was my father's son—or even that he suspected he might be. He applied for a job in the Alcolar Corporation—got it—and then worked for my father for a while, biding his time and waiting to see what was what.'

She slicked a nervous tongue over painfully dry lips and Jake suddenly thought that he saw the way that this was going.

'And what *was* what? I take it you met him then?'

Her nod was silent, her eyes troubled.

'I—I didn't know who he was and I was only a kid at the time. Barely seventeen. I—developed a huge crush on him.'

'For a huge crush, read—you thought you were in love with him,' Jake inserted when she froze, seeming to find it impossible to go on.

Mercedes looked as if she wished she could refute the comment angrily, but it was obvious that she couldn't.

'He didn't treat you badly?'

If this damn brother had behaved to her in the Alcolar way—if he had broken her heart—then he would have words with him. More than words.

'Alex?' It was obvious from her tone that he was on the wrong track. 'Not at all! In fact, it was my behaviour that forced him to come out into the open about who he was before he was really ready. He couldn't have been kinder— or gentler about it. And anyway, even if I hadn't been his sister, he'd already met the one woman who could ever be his wife.'

'The woman he's married to now?'

She nodded agreement.

'Louise. They're totally happy together.'

Totally happy in the way that she and Jake could never be. She didn't have to speak the words; they were there in her voice and in her eyes. But Jake didn't have the time or the space in his thoughts to deal with that consideration right now. Instead, he was thinking of Alex, seeing the other man's face in his thoughts, comparing it with the reflection that he saw in the mirror every day.

Two tall, dark-haired, light-eyed men. Two men with wide cheekbones, firm jaws, full lips. With a lean strength, a powerful frame, long legs… Two men who might almost have been taken for brothers, or at least the cousins that he and Ramón were in reality.

Two men who were alike enough to force the question he didn't want to face into his brain. To make him wonder whether, in him, she had found someone who looked enough like Alex—like her forbidden brother—to act as a stand-in for the man she couldn't have.

It didn't make for a comfortable feeling. To think that he

wasn't really wanted as himself but as the closest thing that she could get to the man she had once wanted to love.

'You said you frightened yourself. What exactly did you mean by that?'

Her eyes dodged away from his, looked anywhere but at him, refusing to meet his demanding gaze.

'I—don't normally act like that. I'm not someone who rushes into things without thinking… I've always thought of myself as my mother's daughter. When I found out about Ramón and Alex, saw how *Papá*'s irresponsibility had shattered our family—and others—I swore I'd always be careful, always think before I acted. That night I realised that I could be every bit as impulsive and thoughtless as my father, and I panicked.'

And that was as far as she dared to go, Mercedes acknowledged to herself. She didn't have the courage to admit that she had only ever reacted this way with one man—with Jake. Even the time that she had had that mammoth crush on Alex, when she had believed that she was in love then, seemed hopelessly insignificant beside the tidal wave of feeling that had overwhelmed her with Jake.

She had adored Alex—still did—but as her brother. Even when she'd thought he wasn't related to her she had, she saw now, never, ever felt anything like the overpowering force of feeling that had swept her off balance with Jake.

And she had never known such all-consuming sexual desire with any other man in the whole of her life. Never really felt *anything*, if she was honest. She'd always suspected that she was like her brothers, that, when she fell, she would fall hard. That she'd only know one man who could ever claim her as his wife.

And she had fallen hard—harder than she had ever expected. So hard that there was no chance of recovery, no hope of loving anyone else in the same, wholehearted way.

But the man she had fallen for had none of the same feelings for her. And he had certainly no intention of ever claiming her heart and her future. Here and now was all that he wanted and so here and now was all that she could give him.

'It goes with the way I was brought up—the insistence on respectability and reputation. That's why my father was shocked.'

'Not that he has any right to be,' Jake drawled cynically, pushing back his chair and stretching his long limbs lazily. 'Your father isn't exactly any sort of saint himself, with three sons all by different mothers.'

'He'd be the first to admit that.'

'He would?'

Jake looked totally taken aback. Far more so than she would ever have expected he would be. She felt anger rising inside her at the way he clearly thought of her father, without knowing any of the story.

'If you must know, my father has admitted that he was wrong in the way he behaved in the past. But he was young; he was thoughtless—and he's regretted it ever since.'

'Too late,' Jake growled. 'Aren't all the women involved now dead? Did any of them know?'

'He told my mother,' Mercedes put in hastily. 'She knew. Their marriage had started out as an arranged match—a dynastic one—and when Ramón first appeared, claiming *Papá* as his father, naturally it upset everything. My mother was heartbroken—and furious. But I know that they talked, and talked…and in the end they came so much closer.'

'It was still damn hypocritical of him to treat you the way he did that night—at Ramón's wedding.'

'That was different.'

Too mentally uncomfortable now to sit still, Mercedes jumped to her feet and snatched up her handbag.

'I think it's time we were making a move—' she began, but Jake reached up a hand and clamped it tightly around her wrist, holding her still.

'Not so fast,' he said sharply. 'How was it different?'

He was like a terrier who had his teeth into a bone and wouldn't let it go. And by springing to her father's defence, she had taken herself into dangerous territory where it seemed that emotional landmines lurked under the surface wherever she turned, just waiting for her to make a foolish and unwary move.

'It just was.'

'Mercedes…'

His use of her name was low, dangerous, laced with dark warning.

'I have to—'

She never managed the last word. Even as she opened her mouth, drew in a breath to speak, he had leapt to his feet, lithe and fast, and disturbingly overwhelming.

'*Mercedes.*'

It was even more ominous than before.

'*How* was it different?'

If she struggled, his grip just tightened and she was clamped so hard against him that any attempt at fight would just inflame things. The movement would seem intimate, provocative, and not the act of determined rebellion she wanted it to appear. Already her body was reacting to the heat and power of his closeness, the scent of his skin in her nostrils, the warm touch of his breath on her skin.

'Jake…'

Looking into his eyes, she saw the way that their normal ice-blue had darkened as the deep black of his pupils expanded, obliterating all of the paler colour apart from a tiny rim, like an edge of sky, encircling their edges. She could feel the heavy, sonorous thud of his heart under the ribcage that crushed the softness of her breasts, sense the change in his breathing, the sudden inhalation in reaction.

Already the heat of the sun was being forced to pale in comparison to the rush of fire through her blood. The feelings that took possession of her were wild and fierce and primitive, totally unsuited to the bright, open-plan café. They belonged in a curtained room, in the dark of night, the warmth and softness of a big, big bed. And they made her want to reach out, put her hand over his, raise it, bring it from her arms to her breast, to feel its heat and hardness cupping her intimately.

'*How* was it different?' Jake demanded again, the harshness of his tone slashing through the glowing haze, shattering the golden moment in a split second.

She wished she could defy him. Prayed that she could hold out even a moment longer, but those barely blue eyes blazed into hers, seeming to threaten to drag out her soul from her body and expose it to his brutal scrutiny if she so much as resisted. And she knew when those powerful fingers clamped around her arm tightened ominously that she had to answer or face the embarrassing consequences yet again in a very public place.

'Everyone was there,' she tried to prevaricate, hoping that, even at this late point, she could dodge the issue and get away with a half-truth. 'My father knew how they'd all disapproved of Estrella—the way they ostracised her—he didn't want the same for me.'

'And?' Jake prompted harshly when she paused. He was clearly not convinced that that was the only explanation, not prepared to let her leave it at that. 'And?'

'And—and he knew that I'd promised…that I'd promised my mother.'

'Your *mother*?'

It was clearly the last thing that Jake had expected and his head went back sharply, steely eyes narrowing in swift, frowning assessment. Even the hand on her arm loosened a little, easing its bruising grip.

'What the hell did you promise your mother?'

'That…'

There was no hope for it but to give him the truth. No other answer that she could throw at him and still hope to convince. She had no doubt that he would know if she was even economical with the truth. He would read it in her eyes and he would pounce on the betraying flicker of weakness like a hunting hawk swooping down to snatch up a terrified mouse as its prey.

'That I would only ever—sleep—with a man that I loved. That I wouldn't throw my virginity away on someone who wouldn't value it. Someone I didn't care for.'

If she had lifted her hand and brought it down, hard, painfully, on the lean plane of his cheek, then he couldn't have looked more shocked, more stunned. In fact his clear blue eyes suddenly clouded, their keen gaze blurring as if she had actually used real force against him. Then slowly, deliberately, he shook his head.

'No…' he said rawly, his voice fraying at the edges. 'No.'

But before he could finish, before he could say exactly what it was that he was denying, she lost her nerve again. She couldn't bear to hear him continue. Couldn't bear to let him go on in case he said that no, she couldn't love him—because he didn't want her to. That it was the last thing on earth that he had ever thought of happening, the last thing he could ever wish for.

He was horrified at the thought that she might have fallen in love with him.

And so she forced herself to pull her feelings back under her control. Made herself lift her head and look him in the face.

She even managed to flash a brief, brittle and totally meaningless smile.

'Good thing I didn't keep that promise, isn't it—or where would we be? Love has nothing to do with our relationship—does it?'

'No, nothing,' Jake responded in a worryingly strangled

voice. He still looked stunned, as if he had faced some appalling, unknown horror. As if he had looked over the edge of a dangerously high cliff and seen the reality of the long, long fall down.

And that, she forced herself to acknowledge, was why he had only ever said that he wanted her as a *mistress* rather than a lover.

He had no intention—no thought—of ever marrying her. He wanted her, desired her—he might even care for her in his own way. But he didn't *love* her.

She might think of herself as his lover, because she loved him so desperately, but there was no future in it. She would never be more than a mistress to him and it was time that she faced that fact.

'So now do you see why I don't want you to buy me a ring? It would just be a terrible waste of money.'

'I have the money to waste.'

Was she tempted? Jake wondered. He thought he saw a light in her eyes—just for a moment. But then she blinked and it was gone and there was only a strange emptiness, a bleak darkness.

'Don't waste it on me.'

'How could it ever be a waste to give a beautiful woman beautiful jewellery?'

'But it isn't just jewellery. Why should I want a ring to mark something that I know has only a brief lifespan? Something that is bound to come to an end sooner rather than later. It just won't last and we both know it.'

'You could still have a ring.'

'No! A ring like that's nothing but a lie! I don't want that! If I ever let someone put a ring on this finger, I want it to mean something! I want it to be put there by a man who loves me and who I love in return. I want it to be on my finger because I never, ever want it to come off again.

Because I want that ring there—and that man—for the rest of my life.'

Well, that told him, Jake reflected. She couldn't have made things any plainer if she'd tried.

This was a temporary affair, one with no future and no real meaning. She wasn't committed in any way—and she didn't want to be. She was still looking for the love of her life, but for now the passing fling that she was having with him was an enjoyable distraction—nothing more.

Well, that was fine by him. It was the way he'd lived his life until now.

It was okay by him.

It would do for him…

…for now.

He didn't like the way that the words sounded so hollow even in his own thoughts that they failed to convince him that he meant them.

# CHAPTER FIFTEEN

THE month had almost come to an end.

Time had slipped away without Mercedes really noticing. But now the four weeks that Jake had planned on staying in Spain were nearly up. Ramón and Estrella would be back from their honeymoon in three days, and, when they did, then Jake would move out of the apartment.

And then he would go home to England.

Which of course meant that he would leave Mercedes behind.

The problem was that she didn't know whether this parting would be only temporary or if in fact the news of her brother's homecoming marked the beginning of the end for her.

For Jake, she knew, it would be the perfect excuse to back out of their relationship, either openly or by claiming he would keep in touch and then simply letting things slide. Probably the former, knowing Jake. He wasn't the sort of man to dodge issues. If he had a problem he would meet it head-on and deal with it then and there. Remembering the way he had spoken about ending things with Karen, Mercedes knew that when her time came she could expect only the same sort of blunt dismissal, no punches pulled.

Jake resembled her brother Joaquin so much in this. Joaquin who had always made sure that his mistresses never lasted any longer than a year.

Until Cassie. Cassie had crept into her brother's carefully guarded heart and stayed there. And now she was Joaquin's wife, Mercedes' determined bachelor brother the happiest of married men.

And the happiest of fathers-to-be.

Mercedes winced sharply at that thought. Over the past few days a worry that had begun as merely suspicion had hardened into a major concern, now almost a certainty.

She might be pregnant with Jake's child.

She'd tried to tell herself it was too early to worry. That she was simply late. She'd had a lot on her mind and that was what was keeping things from functioning normally.

But she had never, ever been late before.

Not once.

And the worst, the bitter irony was that if she was right, and she was expecting Jake's child, then she thought she knew exactly the moment that the baby had been conceived.

It had to be that first time she and Jake had made love without a condom. When she had woken in his bed that first time, in Ramón's apartment. When she had opened her eyes and looked into his, and known that she loved him. And she had reached for him...

'Mercedes?'

A voice from behind her made her jump and she whirled round from where she had been standing staring out of the window to find that her father had come into the room.

'I just heard from Ramón. He and Estrella will be back with us tomorrow.'

'So soon?'

Mercedes felt the blood drain from her cheeks. She had thought—hoped—that she would have a little longer with Jake before the blow fell.

'You don't look so happy at the thought,' her father teased. 'Not happy to see your brother back again?'

'It isn't that...'

Mercedes' voice failed her and she couldn't go on, but unexpectedly her father seemed to understand.

'If your brother comes back, then your fiancé will be heading home to England, is that it?' he asked in the sort of sympathetic tone that Mercedes had rarely heard from him before. So rarely that it pushed her into unguarded speech.

'I'm afraid…'

She couldn't finish the sentence; couldn't voice her fears. But her father nodded his head in understanding.

'You're afraid that if he goes, everything will change. That he will forget you.'

'Out of sight, out of mind,' Mercedes murmured.

'If he truly loves you, then it won't be like that.'

*If he truly loves you…*

Mercedes closed her eyes against the pain that sentence brought. There was her problem, right there in those five important, emotive words.

*If he truly loves you…*

'Do you doubt the way you feel, is that it?' Juan Alcolar asked quietly.

'Oh, no!'

The words slipped out involuntarily as Mercedes' eyes flew open to look straight into her father's ebony ones.

'No, nothing like that! I love him; I really do. I think I fell in love with him the first moment I saw him.'

'Then you're like your mother in that,' Juan told her sombrely. 'She always said she loved me from the start, but I never valued her enough. Ours was an arranged marriage.'

'I know, *Mamá* told me. She said she adored you but she had to wait until you came to love her.'

Her father sighed, rubbed his hands over his face in a gesture that made her think immediately of Joaquin. Her eldest brother and her father had had their difficult times—probably because they were so alike—but they were growing closer with every day.

'I was stupid. And blind. I'd been so much in love with Marguerite…'

'Ramón's mother?'

'Ramón's mother, yes. And when she died—so soon after

Ramón was born—I went off the rails. Of course Marguerite's family blamed me for her death—they never forgave me, even before they knew Ramón was my child. Her sister hated me—swore she'd have revenge—and I felt terribly guilty too. I was drinking too much—out of control…I did something very stupid…'

Mercedes could only nod in silence. She knew the story now. How her father, mourning the woman he had loved, had gone to England, had a drunken one-night stand with a woman—the result of which had been Alex, the youngest of her three brothers.

'But when I came back home your mother was waiting for me. She took the pathetic mess of a man I was and put me back together again. And at long last I learned what love was really all about. But I'd wasted so much time. We didn't have long enough together.'

He paused, gave a sigh that seemed to come right from the depths of his soul.

'You came out of that reconciliation, *querida*. Whatever other mistakes I've made in my life, that was not one. You were conceived in love, Mercedes, and because of you, your mother and I at last had a chance to try again—to be a real family. So it's Jake's feelings you're not sure of?'

For a second Mercedes could only stare in blank astonishment, not understanding where her father's question had come from. But then she traced back the conversation they had been having and nodded slowly.

'I don't know what he feels.'

'But if he asked you to marry him…'

Juan caught the swift, flashing look she couldn't conceal before she let her eyes drop and stared fixedly at the floor.

'He didn't ask you to marry him.'

'No.'

It was a low, miserable whisper.

'Then why did he say he had?'

'I—I don't know.'

'I do.'

It was another male voice that cut into the conversation, and this time her brother Joaquin was the one who had spoken. Mercedes' eyes flew to his face, saw the serious expression, the thoughtful light in her brother's grey eyes.

'How...?'

'I was there, remember? I was closer to him than anyone—other than Alex. I saw his face—his eyes. He saw you were in trouble and he didn't hesitate. He just rushed in to rescue you—speaking without thinking.'

Was it true? Could it possibly be real? Mercedes found it impossible even to consider the question properly. Her heart was racing so fast that the pounding of blood at her temples was like the effects of a thunderstorm, scrambling her brain. But underneath all the confusion there was one tiny, hopeful thought.

If Jake had come to her rescue—then maybe he cared—just a little. And if she was pregnant, then perhaps, like her father and mother, this baby, the new life they had created between them, might bring them together after all.

'Do you think...?' she tried to ask and Joaquin spread his hands in a gesture of uncertainty.

'The only person who can tell you is Jake himself. You have to ask him.'

Tomorrow Ramón would be back and he would have to move out.

Jake dragged his suitcase out from the back of the wardrobe where he had stored it for the past month and dumped it on the bed, flinging open the lid with a violent gesture.

Whatever happened, he'd have to move out of here. He had to give his cousin and Estrella the privacy a newly married couple deserved. And the truth was that he'd been away from London long enough. His deputy, Mark, had filled in brilliantly, and technology meant that he had been in touch almost as much as if he were in the office—but it was time to get his hands back on the reins properly. And there was nothing keeping him here.

Except Mercedes.

Jake yanked open a drawer, pulled out a bundle of shirts and dropped them carelessly into the case, his attention not on the task at all.

Mercedes.

He had come here to Spain with the intention of getting her out of his system. Instead, all he had succeeded in doing was the exact opposite.

With every day that passed, every time that they made love, he became more and more entangled in his feelings, his need for her. And with every day that passed it seemed that she became more and more distant from him.

So much so that it had become plain that he would do better to give up now, go home, and forget about her.

If he could.

A bundle of underwear followed the shirts, falling haphazardly into the case, and he tossed some shoes in after them.

'Why should I want a ring to mark something that I know has only a brief lifespan?' Mercedes' voice was so clear in his thoughts that he could almost imagine that she were there in the room with him. The memory twisted something sharply inside him—but not the low, deep-down feeling of physical response he was so used to experiencing whenever he was with Mercedes or thought of her. No, more recently, he had started to feel things higher up. In his chest.

At the spot where, if he was fanciful, he would say that his feelings for her had entered his heart.

But it didn't matter a damn where he felt or what he felt. For the past couple of weeks, Mercedes had kept a careful emotional distance from him.

Oh, he might spend the day with her, talk with her, even laugh with her, but somehow the real Mercedes always slipped away, out of reach if he tried to talk of anything more serious, anything that might take them into a future together. Just as she had done when he had talked of buying her a ring, when she had used the occasion to make it plain that she wanted nothing that even hinted at commitment, whether real or pretence, so now she always sidestepped hastily, moving the subject on to some other, less significant topic, making a joke or finding something in a shop window that suddenly interested her.

Or, if they were here, in the apartment, then she would seduce him. And she knew so well just how to do that, that no matter how much he fought against temptation, no matter how hard he tried to resist, he always ended up giving in to the sensual temptation she offered.

At least when he lost himself in sexual ecstasy then the worries and the doubts and the hellish uncertainties were blasted from his mind. For the time that he held her, caressed her, made love to her, he could forget, could push away all other thoughts. But they always came back. He might know Mercedes in the most intimate way that a man could know a woman, he might strip her naked, take her to his bed, bury himself in her warm and yielding body—but there was always some essential part of her that he felt he could never reach, never touch. Some hidden part of her heart—her soul—that would never be his.

And it was that *never* that was driving him away.

If he could have had any hope, any tiny expectation that things might change, then he would stay and fight—and pray that one day he might win.

But in the last few days it seemed that Mercedes had moved even further away from him. Already he was losing her and the 'sooner rather than later' that she had predicted was coming true.

So if he was wise, he would take his cousin's return as the warning that his time was up. He would get out of here while he still had some pride intact, could hold his head up high. He would say goodbye to Mercedes, because only that way could he have a chance of actually doing what she wanted—and leaving her. If he hung on as he wanted to, waiting for her to be the one to say goodbye, he knew that he could never do it. He would probably lose all pride and beg her to reconsider. Put her in a situation that she would hate—and so hate him for causing it.

He was heading to the bathroom to collect his shaving things when the doorbell rang.

'Mercedes!'

No, not now! Not before he had a chance to get a grip on himself. To think of the words he would have to say—to find the strength to say them.

But in spite of everything, his blind, stupid heart would lift in delighted anticipation of just seeing her face, hearing her voice.

And so it tumbled down fast and hard, jolting him with a bitter sense of shock when he saw that the female figure who stood outside was several inches taller than the one he expected, blonde—and over twenty years older.

'Mother! What—what are you doing here?'

Elizabeth Taverner fixed him with her clear blue eyes, looking deep into his face as if she was hunting for some particular information there. He knew that look of old. It spelled trouble for someone and he rather suspected that today that someone was him.

'I came to find out just what's been going on. I've been hearing some ridiculous rumours about you and I wanted to know if they're true.'

To Mercedes' astonishment, the door to Ramón's apartment was very slightly open. It looked as if someone had just stepped inside and let it swing back on its own, not actually making sure that it had closed properly. Just one small push and it opened again silently, leaving her free to step into the hallway if she wanted.

If she dared.

She had set out on the short journey from her father's house to the place that Jake had made his temporary home full of hope and expectation. Buoyed up on the explanation Joaquin had given her, she had determined to do just as her father said, and find the man she loved, talk to him, see if they could work things out.

They *had* to work things out if there was going to be a baby.

But, coming up in the lift to this floor, all her courage seemed to have deserted her, seeping away into the carpet, leaving her feeling shaken and unsure.

And now the sound of voices coming from the living room froze her half in and half out of the door.

If there was someone here with Jake, then she couldn't go through with this. It would be hard enough to talk to him on his own, but if there was someone else—a woman, by the sound of it—then she would have to give up on the idea and come back some other time.

But would she have the courage some other time? She didn't know if she could bring herself to the same point again if she backed down now.

And yet she would have to, if she was ever to know the truth.

But right now the timing was all wrong. Jake had company…

She was backing away, out the door, when she caught the sound of her own name and froze, listening hard.

'Leave Mercedes to me, Mother!' It was Jake's voice, carrying clearly through another half-open door. 'I'll handle things!'

'Of course you will.' The female voice was sharp and
scornful. 'The way you've handled things this far—and got
yourself caught up in this farcical relationship. You want to
be careful, Jake, or these damn Alcolars will ruin your life,
the way they destroyed Marguerite's. You know what they
did to my sister.'

*Marguerite.* The name was like a knife in Mercedes' heart,
bringing with it a host of memories—recollections of the stories of her father's past life, of an English woman called
Marguerite. The woman that Juan Alcolar had loved and lost.
The woman who had borne his child and died just a few
short months later—Ramón's mother.

'Of course Marguerite's family blamed me for her
death—' her father's words thundered inside her head,
drowning out whatever Jake was saying '—they never forgave me. Her sister hated me—swore she'd have revenge...'

*You know what they did to my sister.*

*Her sister hated me—swore she'd have revenge.*

And Jake had called this woman Mother!

Mercedes clutched at the door, holding on tight for support
as she forced herself to stay upright and listen again.

'It's time you put an end to this fake engagement,' Jake's
mother was saying now. 'Get out of there fast before you
find that you're trapped and you can't get away again. After
all, you don't want to find you actually have to *marry* the
woman by mistake!'

'Marry her by mistake?' Jake's voice was harsh and sarcastic. 'No, I can assure you that's something that's never
going to happen.'

# CHAPTER SIXTEEN

MERCEDES had to slap her hand over her mouth to hold back the whimper of distress that almost escaped her. Her grip on the edge of the door tightened, the knuckles on her other hand showing white through her skin, and there was a terrible buzzing in her ears like the sound of a thousand angry bees as her head spun sickeningly and her stomach heaved in protest.

And now, when she was too vulnerable, too weak and least able to bear it, her mind threw a memory at her, clear and brutally vivid, of the moment that Jake had first come up to her, at that party in London, when she had first seen him and if it hadn't been for Antonia's explanations she would never have known who he was.

But he had known.

He had come up to her, cool and calm and totally collected, and he hadn't even hesitated.

'You're Mercedes Alcolar,' he'd said.

Not, 'Are you Mercedes Alcolar?' Not, 'You're Mercedes Alcolar?' the words rising at the end on a question. But, 'You're Mercedes Alcolar.' Cold and flat—a statement, not an enquiry.

He had known exactly who she was and he had targeted her from the beginning. The whole thing had been a plan of revenge, in his mind, from start to finish.

Run! every instinct she possessed screamed at her. Go! Get out of here now, before someone hears you, realises you're here!

But even as she turned a memory suddenly sliced through

175

the wild confusion and misery inside her thoughts, bringing her up short, lifting her head and stiffening her spine.

'Are you going to do it again?'

She could hear Jake's voice as clearly as when he had flung the accusation at her in this apartment—dear God, was it only three weeks ago? 'Are you going to…run out on me without giving me a chance to say anything—to explain…?' But what explanation could there be? Hadn't she heard him with her own ears? Hadn't he made his feelings absolutely plain?

Jake was determined to make sure that he never ended up marrying her. That was clear enough. Wasn't it?

But she still wasn't going to go and leave him and his vindictive mother to it.

She wasn't going to run.

Drawing in a deep, deep, calming breath, Mercedes swallowed hard to ease her achingly dry throat.

If Jake Taverner really hated the idea of marriage to her that much—if he had only ever entered into this fake engagement, only ever seduced her, to have his revenge for something he believed her father had done to his mother's sister all those years ago—then he was going to have to tell her so to her face.

She was done with running away from Jake. She was going in there to face him once and for all.

Tossing back her hair, she slicked a nervous tongue over painfully dry lips, forced herself to take a step forward…and another…

Jake heard the door swing open behind him, but for a moment he thought it was nothing but the effects of a draught. But then he saw his mother's eyes move, her gaze going over his shoulder, her expression telling him that someone had come into the room.

'Who?'

But even as he spun round he knew.

There was only one person, other than Ramón, who would appear so unexpectedly in the apartment. Only one person who could put that expression of disbelief, anger and—yes— a strange uncertainty on his mother's face.

Mercedes.

But Mercedes looking as he had never seen her before.

She wore a long white halterneck dress that clung to every curve, every contour of her body, but her beautiful face was haggard and drawn, the delicate skin having no colour at all. Her eyes were huge, clouded, dark as coals above the ashen cheeks and her mouth, normally so soft and lushly curved, was drawn tight and cruelly compressed as if to make sure that she never, ever said another word.

She looked as if she had been to hell and back and if he hadn't known it already, then he would have known in that moment just how much he loved her.

'Mercedes…'

Her name escaped on a breath as soft and low as a sigh, but she caught it and she turned to face him.

And she gave him that Alcolar look.

Her spine stiffened. Her jaw tightened. Her chin came up and she stared straight down her aristocratic little nose at him in an expression of the utmost contempt.

*Trying* for an expression of the utmost contempt.

Because now he was so sensitive to her, so aware of her many moods, the multi-faceted persona that was Mercedes Alcolar, that he saw the tiny, giveaway signs he hadn't recognised in the past.

He saw the glistening sheen on those wide dark eyes, the fight she had to keep her mouth from quivering, the brutal control that was fraying at the edges even as she struggled to impose it.

And that was when he knew that she had heard. She had overheard his conversation with his mother and now she was here to let him know exactly what she thought of him.

'I wouldn't have had it happen like this,' he said intently, holding her eyes with his, his mother completely forgotten behind him. 'Not for all the world.'

'No?'

It was cold and brittle as ice, and, if it was possible, her head actually went even higher, her mouth even tighter.

'Then how *did* you plan it to happen? At another family party—some sort of public event?'

'No...'

'Or perhaps you actually thought you'd take it to the absolute limit—is that it, Jake? Were you aiming for the most effect possible—for the time when you could really humiliate me?'

*Humiliate.*

The word exploded in his face with the force of a landmine. He hadn't been expecting that. Poor, blind, stupid fool that he was, he had looked into her face, and thought he had interpreted her expression—but he hadn't known the half of it. He really hadn't seen *this* coming.

And of course he should have done. She was an Alcolar after all.

'You'd find my proposal a *humiliation*?'

It hurt even to say it. It twisted in his guts and threatened to rip them from his body.

But at the same time as he spoke, she demanded, 'Exactly when were you going to jilt me—at the altar?'

Their words clashed, froze, seemed to hang in the air as they stared at each other, blue eyes locking tight with deep, deep brown.

'Humiliation?' she asked.

'Jilt you?'

And then suddenly, slowly, eyes still holding, they both shook their heads in denial of the accusatory words.

'No!'

This time it was impossible even to tell which one had

spoken or that they both had. The single word echoed as one in a harsh, deep masculine voice, and her lighter, but no less intense tone.

'Jake…'

It was his mother who spoke, reminding him at last that she was still in the room. And suddenly he thought he saw exactly what was wrong.

His mother saw Mercedes as the enemy, and it radiated from her. With Elizabeth in the room, there was no way that Mercedes was ever going to speak the truth, or tell him how she really felt.

With an effort he dragged his gaze away from Mercedes' stunned stare, striding past her to the door. Holding it open wide.

'Mother—out.'

It was a command, hard and rough, his feelings too raw to allow him to soften his tone.

'Please,' he added belatedly. 'I need to be alone with Mercedes.'

Don't argue with me, the look he gave Elizabeth said. Don't fight me on this or make me choose, because you won't like my answer if you do.

And he breathed a sigh of relief as he saw the tight, argumentative expression on her face melt and she turned a slow, considering glance on Mercedes' face before doing as he asked and walking out of the room.

He even thought that she murmured, 'Good luck,' in the faintest whisper as she passed him.

Jake shut the door firmly behind her, and stood for a moment, his eyes closing briefly before he turned slowly to face Mercedes again.

'Now…' he said as firmly and as calmly as he could manage. 'Just what is all this about?'

'What is all this about?'

Mercedes couldn't believe he was asking the question.

Hadn't he heard a single thing she was saying? Did he think that she was deaf as well as stupid?

'I heard what you said.'

'I know.'

His blue-eyed gaze didn't flicker but held hers with a burning intensity that made it impossible to look away. 'You made that obvious.'

'Well, then…'

'Was it so bad? So totally appalling?'

'You have to ask? You stand there and say…say that you're determined you'll never end up marrying me—and then you ask, you dare to ask, *Was it so bad?*'

'No—' Jake interjected but, lost in her pain and misery, she was beyond listening.

'Do you know how it felt to hear you say that? To know that all of this was just a scheme—just a plan for revenge?'

'Mercedes—'

'I realise now that you probably just planned on seducing me and then discarding me at first. If I hadn't run out on you, then you would have got away with it. Perhaps you even planned to—to destroy two birds with the one stone. Perhaps I was to be used to teach your Karen a lesson too—show her that she too was dumped—in the same moment that you showed me how little I meant to you.'

'No—'

'But I got away from you then. I foiled your plan, frustrated your callous need for revenge by running away. And so you came after me, looking for more—and I gave you the opportunity, poor, blind, besotted fool that I was. I fell straight into your arms and let you do as you wanted with me.'

'Not straight.' Jake's tone was wry and to her total disbelief there was actually a half smile on his stunning face. 'You fought me a bit first.'

'But not enough! I let you use me—hurt me—let you wreak revenge on my family—'

'Mercedes, no!'

Jake's composure had shattered totally, his hands flying up in the air in a non-English gesture of denial and defence.

'No, no, no, no, *no*!'

He marched across the room towards her, grabbing hold of her hands and holding them tight, blue eyes burning into brown, his face only inches away from her own.

'It isn't like that—it was never like that, believe me. I never came after you for revenge but because I couldn't help myself. I couldn't stay away from you, couldn't get you out of my head. You *have* to believe me!'

'W-why?'

She wanted it to come out strong and defiant, demanding an answer, but there was something in his expression, in the force of his grip on her hands, that drained all the strength from her voice and made it shake shamefully, betraying the effect she didn't want him to know he was having on her.

'Why do I have to believe you?'

'Because if you feel this way then you didn't hear things properly. If you believe that I said I was never going to marry you, then you didn't hear right—and you didn't hear *everything* I said.'

'Everything?'

Her tongue stumbled over the word and there was a hard, tight knot of emotion clogging her throat. It was appalling how much she wanted to believe him. That intent blue gaze said that she could trust him.

'You can't have heard it right.' Jake took pity on her struggle to speak. 'Because what I said was that marrying you *by mistake* was the thing I wouldn't do. And you can't have heard it *all*, because what I said then was that when I ask the woman I love to marry me, I intend to do it very much

on purpose. I want everyone to know that it's not a mistake—
but the thing that I most want in all the world.'

'You can't have heard it *all*…'

Mercedes was back outside the door, hearing Jake's
words—hearing them *again* inside her head, with the very
different interpretation that Jake had put on them. And then
there had been that buzzing, whirling noise inside her head
when for a moment she had thought that she might pass
out—and…and…

*And she hadn't been able to hear any other thing!*

If Jake had said…

*When* Jake had said…

And she was remembering now the way that he had said,
'You'd find my proposal a *humiliation*?' There had been such
a raw note on the last word, one that had turned it into a
sound of pain as cruel and as bitter as anything she had been
experiencing.

'The woman that you— Who…?'

The touch of Jake's hands on hers eased. He was no longer
crushing them with the force of the need to have her believe,
but holding them safe and firm, his grip gentle but strong as
if he would never let her go.

'Who do you think, sweetheart? The woman I love is you.
The only woman in the world I want to marry is you. That's
the real truth—always has been. It's just that at first I was
too blind to see it. When I said I couldn't get you out of my
mind, I never realised that the real truth was that I couldn't
get you out of my *heart*. I love you, Mercedes. Can you
believe that?'

How could she believe anything else? It was there in his
eyes, in his face, in his smile, so gentle and tender that it was
like being bathed in the soft, golden glow of the sun.

'Yes… Yes, I can.'

It was an effort to speak and her voice was thick and rough

as the knot in her throat melted and her heart, which had seemed to be frozen all this time, began to flutter in her chest.

Tears were blurring her eyes but they were tears of joy and happiness, no longer tears of pain. She blinked them away furiously so that she could see his face and the change that came over it as she found the strength to speak again.

'I can believe it—because the only man in the world I want to marry is you. I think I fell in love with you that first night—that's why I acted so much out of character. But I didn't know that—and I scared myself. Love is scary, isn't it, when you don't know what's happening to you? But I know now, that's why I can say—I love you, Jake. More than words can say.'

The look on his face was everything she had ever dreamed it would be. And as she met his glowing eyes, saw the smile of love widen, deepen, she knew that the happiness that was etched into every stunning feature was matched and mirrored in her own expression.

At last Jake released her hands and his arms came round her, gathering her close, holding her up against him until it was impossible to tell where she ended and he began. Looking down into her face with eyes that were so dark they were no longer blue, but almost all black as night, he smiled again.

'Then let's not try with words—will this tell you how I feel?'

His kiss was all she had ever dreamed of and more. It was a kiss of such tenderness, such devotion that the happy tears she had been struggling with finally broke through her control and spilled out of her eyes, tumbling down her cheeks to be kissed away by Jake's softly caressing mouth.

'Sweetheart, I know we've done a lot of this the wrong way round—we were engaged before I ever proposed—but now I want to do things right. I love you more than the world and I want to spend the rest of my days with you, grow old with you, share my life with you. Will you marry me—be my wife—have my children?'

'Yes.'

It was low, deeply heartfelt with all the emotion she could put into the single word.

'Yes, I will marry you. I would love to be your wife—have your children...'

A sudden thought struck her, the memory of why she had come here in the first place, and a new and very different sort of smile broke through the tears as she laughed up into his beloved face.

'Although, my darling, if my suspicions are right, then I think that that's something else we've done the wrong way round.'

Introducing a brand-new miniseries

For _Love_ OR
MONEY

_This is romance on the red carpet..._

For Love or Money is the ultimate reading experience
for the reader who has a taste for tales of wealth and
celebrity and the accompanying gossip and scandal!

Look out for the special covers.

Coming in December:

# TAKEN BY THE HIGHEST BIDDER
### _by Jane Porter_

#2508

_Harlequin Presents®_
_The ultimate emotional experience!_

HARLEQUIN®
_Presents_

Seduction and Passion Guaranteed!

www.eHarlequin.com                    HPFLOMCED

## THE F●RTUNES OF TEXAS: *Reunion*

**The price of privilege—the power of family.**

Keeping Her Safe
# Myrna Mackenzie

"Nothing scares me…except losing control of my life."
—Natalie McCabe,
investigative journalist

Natalie McCabe witnesses a murder, and when the man responsible escapes from jail, she finds herself in grave danger. Fortunately her new bodyguard, Vincent Fortune, has the brawn to keep her safe. But can he protect her from his own desire?

On sale in December.

*Where love comes alive*™

**Visit Silhouette Books at www.eHarlequin.com**     FOTRKHS

not read.

If you enjoyed what you just read,
then we've got an offer you can't resist!

## Take 2 bestselling love stories FREE!

## Plus get a FREE surprise gift!

**Clip this page and mail it to Harlequin Reader Service®**

**IN U.S.A.**
3010 Walden Ave.
P.O. Box 1867
Buffalo, N.Y. 14240-1867

**IN CANADA**
P.O. Box 609
Fort Erie, Ontario
L2A 5X3

**YES!** Please send me 2 free Harlequin Presents® novels and my free surprise gift. After receiving them, if I don't wish to receive anymore, I can return the shipping statement marked cancel. If I don't cancel, I will receive 6 brand-new novels every month, before they're available in stores! In the U.S.A., bill me at the bargain price of $3.80 plus 25¢ shipping & handling per book and applicable sales tax, if any*. In Canada, bill me at the bargain price of $4.47 plus 25¢ shipping & handling per book and applicable taxes**. That's the complete price and a savings of at least 10% off the cover prices—what a great deal! I understand that accepting the 2 free books and gift places me under no obligation ever to buy any books. I can always return a shipment and cancel at any time. Even if I never buy another book from Harlequin, the 2 free books and gift are mine to keep forever.

106 HDN DZ7Y
306 HDN DZ7Z

Name _____ (PLEASE PRINT)

Address _____ Apt.#

City _____ State/Prov. _____ Zip/Postal Code

*Not valid to current Harlequin Presents® subscribers.*

*Want to try two free books from another series?*
*Call 1-800-873-8635 or visit www.morefreebooks.com.*

\* Terms and prices subject to change without notice. Sales tax applicable in N.Y.
\*\* Canadian residents will be charged applicable provincial taxes and GST.
  All orders subject to approval. Offer limited to one per household.
  ® are registered trademarks owned and used by the trademark owner and or its licensee.

PRES04R                                    ©2004 Harlequin Enterprises Limited

# eHARLEQUIN.com

## The Ultimate Destination for Women's Fiction

### Visit eHarlequin.com's Bookstore today for today's most popular books at great prices.

- An extensive selection of romance books by top authors!
- Choose our convenient "bill me" option. No credit card required.
- New releases, Themed Collections and hard-to-find backlist.
- A sneak peek at upcoming books.
- Check out book excerpts, book summaries and Reader Recommendations from other members and post your own too.
- Find out what everybody's reading in Bestsellers.
- Save BIG with everyday discounts and exclusive online offers!
- Our Category Legend will help you select reading that's exactly right for you!
- Visit our Bargain Outlet often for huge savings and special offers!
- Sweepstakes offers. Enter for your chance to win special prizes, autographed books and more.

**Your purchases are 100% guaranteed—so shop online at www.eHarlequin.com today!**

INTBB104R

**Seduction and Passion Guaranteed!**

# Jet Set Wives

## GLITZ. GLAMOUR. PARTIES. PASSION.

Don't miss the last book in this hot new trilogy
from Harlequin Presents® bestselling author

# *Penny Jordan*

Penny Jordan has an outstanding record: over 150
novels published, some of which have hit the
*New York Times* bestseller list.

Now join Penny in traveling to glamorous locations and
follow the exciting lives of these jet-set couples!

### Coming in December 2005:

## BLACKMAILING THE SOCIETY BRIDE

### #2505

In case you missed them:

### August 2005:

## BEDDING HIS VIRGIN MISTRESS

### #2481

### October 2005:

## EXPECTING THE PLAYBOY'S HEIR

### #2495

**www.eHarlequin.com**                              HPJSW2

# Coming Next Month

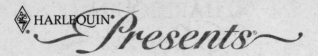

HARLEQUIN *Presents*

## THE BEST HAS JUST GOTTEN BETTER!

### #2505 BLACKMAILING THE SOCIETY BRIDE Penny Jordan
*Jet-Set Wives*
Lucy was facing huge debts after divorcing her cheating husband.
Millionaire Marcus Canning needed an heir—and a wife. Lucy knew
Marcus wanted her for convenience—but she'd always loved him, and
she couldn't resist his passionate lovemaking....

### #2506 THE GREEK'S CHRISTMAS BABY Lucy Monroe
*Christmas theme*
Greek tycoon Aristide Kouros has a piece of paper to prove that
he's married, but no memory of his beautiful wife, Eden. Eden loves
Aristide and it's breaking her heart that he has no recollection of their
love. But Eden has a secret that will bind Aristide to her forever....

### #2507 SLEEPING WITH A STRANGER Anne Mather
*Foreign Affairs*
Helen Shaw's holiday on the island of Santos should be relaxing. But
then she sees Greek tycoon Milos Stephanides. Years ago they had an
affair—until, discovering he was untruthful, Helen left him. Now she
has something to hide from Milos....

### #2508 TAKEN BY THE HIGHEST BIDDER Jane Porter
*For Love or Money*
In Monte Carlo Baroness Samantha van Bergen has been wagered—
and won by darkly sexy Italian racing driver Cristiano Bartolo. Virginal
Sam is scared Cristiano will seduce her—but she quickly discovers he
has another reason for wanting her. Bedding her is just a bonus...!

### #2509 HIS WEDDING-NIGHT HEIR Sara Craven
*Wedlocked!*
Since fleeing her marriage to Sir Nicholas Tempest, Cally Maitland has
become accustomed to life on the run. But Nicholas isn't prepared
to let Cally go. He has a harsh ultimatum: give him their long-overdue
wedding night—and provide him with an heir!

### #2510 CLAIMING HIS CHRISTMAS BRIDE Carole Mortimer
*Christmas theme*
When Gideon Webber meets Molly Barton he wants her badly. But
he is convinced she is another man's mistress....Three years later
a chance meeting throws Molly back in his path, and this time he's
determined to claim her—as his wife.